SIX
BULLETS

Jason Ewen

This book is dedicated to:

Donald Ewen

Mary Ewen

Haldon Ewen

Fiona Ewen

Clinton Ewen

Table of Contents

Introduction

Thank you for purchasing my Book. I hope you will enjoy this mystery which touches on many themes and characters. The book is intended for readers aged between nine and ninety. All should find it easy to read.

The book delves into people's character and the deeds they have done. I have lived a life full of change. Understanding people as I do and observing their drives, emotions, longings and needs. This book is written to enjoy the different social backgrounds and the influences it can have.

The importance of knowing who we are as people and allowing bad thoughts to become deeds. Writing this book has made me realise we can all be better if we follow our dreams. Some people like a read during their lunch hour, when they are at work. This book will take you on a journey far away from the hum drum life that surrounds us all and into a world of Majic, Mystery, Romance, Deceit, Daring and hidden personalities. The ideal partner which baffles in its offerings of intrigue. A dull, repetitive journey to work, in a taxi or on the, bus, train or a flight suddenly becomes a pleasure.

Get comfy then read in bed, read in the bath, read in the garden or read in your favorite chair. Whatever it is let this book be your perfect companion.

Chapter 1: Leaving Home

Pedro Sanchez thoughts drifted in and out of the incident that had happened on the previous evening. He did not want to but his mind thought back on the night it had happened and he contemplated the event. Last evening, he sat outside on his stool where he sat every night but this night was different. With no moon for light, it was black as pitch. Suddenly Pedro thought he heard a sound as he sat in the darkness. He listened again but this time more intently and he heard the sound again. It was a cutting or scraping noise coming from the corner of the field. He grabbed the four-pronged fork and carried it behind his back moving slowly and silently.

As Pedro got to the corner of the field, he saw a man filling several hessian sacks and stealing their vegetables. Pedro did not want or anticipate any trouble. His thoughts turned to simply giving the thief a few choice words and telling him not to return. He began by saying "who are you and what are you doing"? The man straightened up and lunged at him with the knife he had been using to cut the vegetables. Die he said venomously. Pedro stepped to one side but the thief still slashed through his shirt leaving a gash which began to bleed through his shirt. Bringing the fork from behind his back he held it tight and without thinking ran the man straight through his chest. The thief made a few gurgling noises then fell backwards on to the soil. Pedro threw the fork into the ground next to him. Saying under his breath Forgive me Dear Lord, I did not mean for this thing to happen.

He thought whatever shall I do. He realised he must deal with this for the sake of his family. Being in jail or worse would not help anyone he even thought of going to the Civil Guard and telling them what he had done. He stood and turned to go back to the farm house for a shovel. He returned shortly and began digging as he could see the thief was dead. He dug until the makeshift grave had sides that were above his head he climbed out and rolled the body of the thief into the grave and began filling it in with his shovel. Finally, he used his shovel to hit the ground hard compacting it down and laying fresh soil over it to make it look like the rest of the field.

He walked back to the farm house and ran the outside tap washing himself all over and retired to bed. It was soon morning and he went down to breakfast at his usual time. His mother told him to take some warn soup to his father which he did. Then shouted from the top of the stairs mother, mother please come up here. His mother entered the room and went pale as she saw her husband laying on his back with one arm trailing out of the bed and he was dead. Pedro lifted his arm feeling a coldness in it as he replaced it under the cover. His mother sobbed saying come downstairs and get your breakfast before it gets cold. They sat at the table in silence for what must have seemed like an age. Eventually his mother spoke saying well we knew he didn't have long. Pedro agreed with a few nods of his head. They sat there together for a long while without speaking. Then a loud knock came from the door, his mother's face was distorted with shock. Pedro got up and opened the door to see a man in a dark blue suit standing there. Good morning the visitor said I am from the bank in town. I have come to ask you to pay the six hundred and sixty-six Passatas you owe us. Pedro's mother said we haven't got it. Well, what to do the man from the bank said. What can we do Pedro's mother asked. The choices are limited he replied you can pay us now in full and I can return to the bank until next time I visit, Pedro's mother said or what else. Well, he said trying to smile you could always let the bank take the property over. There would be no need to worry anymore, we at the bank call it "pay or go". Pedro's mother said what other choices do we have. The man from the bank stated quite frankly none, you would have to move out one month from now. This grace is given by the bank which appreciates your long custom. Pedro and his mother looked at each other. Pedro knew only too well they could not even raise half that sum so the only course left open to them was to vacate the farm house and return the property to the bank. His mother could see what he was thinking and said right that settles it, you may collect the keys in one months' time. With that the man from the bank wasted no time shaking her hand and left. Whatever next she cried. Pedro said I am sorry mother. She replied we do not have anything to be sorry for we will see if anything turns up in the next month, full well knowing nothing would. Pedro said in his most cheerful voice well I must tend to the field. Three weeks later his mother died of influenza leaving Pedro to find somewhere else to live. So, he just walked away. He took all the biscuits his mother had made together with a loaf bread from the kitchen and set off with three dollars in his pocket.

Pedro Sanchez walked up a steep hill on a sandy dusty road when he crested the top it flattened out for a quarter of a mile. At the side of the road on a fallen tree sat an old man. Come, come sit the old man said tapping the log beside him. Pedro stood at his feet and bent his legs as he grabbed his knees for support to bend deeply. As he looked closely at the old man's face, he realised he was blind, his eyes were a milky white colour and the lids had turned upwards. Do you mind if I touch your face he said. Pedro obliged and lent forward. The old man said youth, I remember that with a smile. Pedro asked where is this place? The old man gave a cryptic answer saying it's here, there and its nowhere, do you see the goats in the field over there. Yes, Pedro answered, what about them? Can you see the black one? "Yes". Well, that is the Judas goat. Oh, Pedro said not knowing what he was talking about. It is the Judas goat because late at night when thieves come it leads a small bunch of goats away from the others to the corner of the field. When the thieves see them huddled in the corner, they hold a fence in place and quickly open a small piece of it to let the Judas goat out. One of them slaughters the goats and when it is done, they dump them in the cart. Oh, dear Pedro said how horrible, as he looked at the road in front of him asking what's further down there? The old man said that leads to evil, put it out of your mind. And where you have come from leads to salvation. Beware young one. That is the only advice I have to offer you. Pedro stood and reached into his bag offering the old man on of his biscuits which the old man put in his jacket pocket. Farewell my friend Pedro shouted as he walked away.

It was a scorchingly hot late September afternoon just as Pedro Sanchez entered Veracruz old town in the summer of 1834. The heat was unbearable - even for Pedro Sanchez. Pedro was a wiry six feet and one inch made of all muscle and bone. His black hair stuck out. And his keen eyes shone out like blue marbles from under the tortured straw hat he wore. Pedro raised his head and looked from under the brim of his hat.

The street was deserted apart from a bunch of tumbleweed crossing the street further down and made their way from one side of the road to the other Pedro stood in the quiet of the day. It was like the world had ended total in silence. His long journey and the heat had made him feel slightly disorientated. He started to cross the dusty road to the saloon. He looked at the creaking old wooden door hanging on one hinge as if crying out for someone to fix it. Faded and peeling paint read what was left of the name of the saloon, he could only make out three of the words "DIABLO WAITS SALOON" which he dismissed.

The heat of the day made him want to look for shade so Pedro crossed the dusty road and made straight for the shelter of the saloon. He pushed the one good door. Inside seemed dark, finally his eyes adjusted from the bright sunlight outside.

Entering the saloon Pedro saw two large card tables in the first bay window to his left that was full and to the right three smaller tables in the other dirty bay window which was full. He also scanned the room and noticed there was only seat across from what looked like an old man with a wide brimmed Stetson hat which was pulled tightly on his head with the brim tipped forward which made his features fall into shadow.

Pedro walked across the room and sat in the chair opposite the old man. He had not wanted to move from the farm and did not want the events that had befallen him but never the less they happened and here he was. A pretty waitress came up to his table and said "what can I get you"? Pedro stated two beers, the old man waved a hand in cancellation, then seemed as if his mind had suddenly been changed and he waved towards the waitress. The Waitress walked away but knew the drinks order would stand. The old man said "tell me son what brings you these parts"? Pedro honestly answered I left my home and walked for a long time and then I was here. My home was my father's farm. The old man said "was". Pedro did not understand why he was telling a complete stranger why his story it just felt right. The old man said so you were behind a plough sheer. Pedro looked somewhat bemused and simply said yes since I was eleven years old that was our only income for the farm. The drinks arrived.

I walked for a long time then I was here. My home was my father's farm. The old man said "was". Pedro did not understand why he was telling a complete stranger why his story it just felt right. The old man said so you were behind a plough sheer. Pedro looked somewhat bemused and simply said yes since I was eleven years old that was our only income for the farm. The drinks arrived. Pedro wondered about the curious sign on the door to the right of them which had been burnt into the side facing them. Pedro said can you tell me "What does it mean" pointing at the door? The old man answered " it means what it says. The sign also stated $1 entrance fee, No Guns, Knives or other armaments! 'Remember' the greatest of riches lay beyond this door.

Pedro was intrigued and he said what do you get if you win the challenge. The old man raised his head a little and looked from under the brim of his hat. Then he mysteriously answered the answers to your question are on the other side of the door. Pedro questioned, have you ever. been through the door, the old man cryptically told him, no names no questions and definitely no answers

Pedro changed the subject and said oh it's a hot one today and I'm used to working in the fields so heat doesn't usually bother me but today seems so warm. The old man said it is hot Veracruz town all year round you get used to it or you die. Pedro said in reply said yes, I see, which he didn't. Pedro sat for nearly an hour thinking. Pedro though about what had driven him to end up in the place and now he was here, wherever here was. Finally breaking off from his thoughts he looked at the old man's craggy face. The old man said put all thoughts of the challenge out of you mind it is a fool's errand, make your way back to your farm. Pedro looked down at his knees and said my parents are both dead and the farm is now owned by the bank. I have nothing to go back to. The old man sighed and said I give you this advice freely do not enter that place pointing at the heavy door. Pedro wondered about the curious sign on the door to the right of them which had been burnt into the side facing them. Pedro said can you tell me "What does it mean" pointing at the door. The old man answered " it means what it says. Pedro saw burnt into the door witing which announced 'Remember' the greatest of riches lay beyond this door. He was puzzled as all who had gone through it had been.

He was intrigued and he said what do you get if you win the challenge. Then mysteriously the old man told Pedro the answers to your question are on the other side of the door. Pedro questioned, have you ever been through the door. The old man simply said, no names no questions and definitely no answers.

6

Pedro said "yes I understand" when it was clear had no understanding what so ever. Pedro changed the subject and said oh it's a hot one today and I'm used to working in the fields so heat doesn't usually bother me but today seems so warm. The Old town is made up of three buildings, the Church, the Castle and here adding it is hot in Veracruz old town all year round you get used to it or you die. Pedro said in reply said yes, I see, which he didn't. Thank you, Pedro, said. Then without warning Pedro kicked back his chair and made for the door.

Chapter 2: Rose

Rose rarely if ever spoke about the subject of her upbringing. She needed the job and the opportunity seemed too good to be missed. However, she thought to herself of those times when she would have liked to have ended it all. But it broke out of here like a hole in a dam. Thinking about how she had been abused by her parents. Her father would take his leather belt to Rose several times each week. What had you done Pin asked? I would be beaten by him for taking too long to bring the bread from the town or not carrying out enough chores around the house. One time he beat me until I bled Rose told him, it was for not sitting up straight at the table but he didn't realise that I had twisted a muscle in my back from his earlier beating and was unable to. How did your mother react to this treatment Pin enquired. She was if anything worse than him. She would scold and torment me and when my father came home, he would get a kind of enjoyment out of my beating. My mother seemed satisfied that she incited my father to deal with me and allow her when desire had conceived with a sense of detachment, allowing it give birth to her sins. She would tell my father to scold and curse me for the vagabond I was. My father shouted Bastardo meaning I was illegitimate and my mother added they never wanted me. She said you eat our food and you are a lazy and disobedient girl. One day not long after this she was trying to get to sleep on my floor upstairs. When the thought entered my mind, what if I ran away and did not tell them where I was going and what if they were unable to chase me or raise the alarm with the Civil Guard that I was missing. They would surely put an end to me if I was brought back.

Mr Pin I will recount the tale of how I came to be here. I want someone to know my deeds and why I did it. I think your judgement will be fair in your decision to offer me this position. Pin replied please tell me everything in detail.

One morning I was half filled with dread and half filled with anticipation. In the afternoon Mr Pin, my mother said go to the town and bring bread. I slipped the knife that sat on the kitchen table into my smock and said yes mother as she replied and don't be long or your father will deal with you. I walked behind her the grabbed hold of her hair, pulled her head back and cut deeply into her throat. I pushed her head forward, rested it on her chest and leant her over the sink in a natural pose as though she was cleaning vegetables. Pin asked what did you do then. I sat and waited for over half an hour she told him, finally my father came through the door, he was a stocky man who was very strong. He plumped down on his usual seat at the table and began by recalling his day at work and asked how was you day addressing his wife as neither of them had any interest in my day. Neither of them usually spoke to Rose except to chastise her for some misdemeanour. Are you all right. He shouted. No answer came as he began rising from his chair. I struck him deep in his back and he tried to reach over his shoulder to take hold of the knife. But I quickly withdrew it and stabbed him once again lower down. The third strike was so deep that an inch of the knifes tip broke off and lodged under his backbone.

Cleaning the knife on my mother's skirt I rolled up her clean smock and removed it from her. I fastened the two strings at either side of my shoulders so the straps could make a hammock for anything I needed to carry. I dragged my fathers' dead body behind my mother's body lying over the sink. I then took the knife and washed the blood off it. I got hold of my fathers' hand and forced the knifes handle into his palm and wrapped his finger tightly around it. I hoped the Civil Guard would think my mother had stabbed him but he was so strong he took the knife and stabbed her. I cleaned and scrubbed the floor of the kitchen, taking extra care to clean the chair and floor all around where her father earlier been sitting. She checked round one last time and she then wrote a note to her mother saying I will be back after I have been to the market, love you and see you later and placed it on the kitchen table.

I left around an hour later and headed for the cool house where apples were stored. She collected enough to fill her smock and I headed for the town.

Going towards the town she passed two women who knew who I was and said hello Rosetta. The town was busy and people were engaged in looking at what was on the market stalls. As Thursday was market day the market that helped me wind my way behind the crowds while buying a loaf of bread from a seller, I made for a street on the left which led off round a corner to quiet part of town. The heat was getting unbearable and after checking the street was clear I drank as much as could from the fountain in the square then soaked my hair as I had no means of carrying any of the water with me. Night fell around ten O' clock when the streets were quiet and deserted. I carried on walking then stopped and forced my way under the bushes about a mile away from the fountain. Early morning found me dishevelled but not disheartened. I had a nourishing breakfast of apple and bread which I had bought the day before from the market. I looked out at the opposite side of the bushes and was surprised to see green fields falling away steeply down a mountain side and stopping at a dusty track. She walked all day and well into the evening and then settled down with bread and apple and lay next to the hedge which was separated by a steep dusty road which from the side I had seen from the top of the hill in the early morning.

A lite morning wind woke me from my sleep. So, I checked for anyone who might be around. There was no one anywhere in sight. Rose got up and climbed over a gate and made for the road noticing there were many rocky outcrops that met the road from the mountains. I thought they would make good cover if she needed to get off the road quickly. I walked with this in mind until

I came across a church near the bottom of the road. Rose watched intently but seeing no one had gone in or out of the church decided she would take a risk and run down the dust track until it met the road which was bit wider but more of the same dusty track.

Finally, I carried on until coming to this saloon and I saw the large notice on your door. I don't know if you remembered exactly what it reads, it was asking for a bargirl with the final words simply instructing anyone to ask inside. I could hardly believe my eyes as this is what I wanted and needed and I will give your patrons my very best service each and every day. I though was this divine intervention, luck or fate? Whatever it was I was grateful for it and I am not about to turn this position down. Mr Pin declared wonderful and smiled to show he was pleased with what Rose had divulged to him. Incase you might have been wondering Mr Pin, I taught myself to read from the three books I owned which I found on a wall some years ago in the town. One was a book called The Bible another was Mathematics Understood and a third book was by Daniel Defoe and was a story of a man called Robinson Crusoe.

Chapter 3: The Challenge

The heavy door was made of what looked like Oak with a frame of iron and large iron nails protruded through the frame from the inside of the door. It reminded him of an illustration he had seen in a book. It was the type of door you might find on a large sea going clipper ship or a Castle. He opened the door and two large men blocked his return after closing the door. Pedro took his last and only dollar out of his jacket pocket and handed it to one of the two men and they took up their previous positions against the iron door and pointed down the long dark passageway. He could see nothing as he felt his way by one side of the cold damp cave wall. Eventually a bend came up and he felt his way round to see a burning torch above another door in the distance which looked like first one, so he entered through. As he reached the door, he outstretched his hand and suddenly the door opened. Pedro entered and turned round to see to his amazement no one stood at either side of the door. He turned back to see over a hundred men ten deep in a circle. Pedro made his way through them to find a large round circular table which held a huge mountain of money in the centre. Men were throwing money onto the pile. At the of the table opposite to the gamblers was a thin faced China man wearing a crown on a elevated chair looking directly down over proceedings at the table. Sat next to him was a dwarf who looked like he was made of sheer muscle and he was wearing a smaller crown. Pedro had never seen anything like it in his short life. He didn't know what to make of the scene before him.

In a very short time, an announcement was made by the dwarf "All here should know the rules" and most of them did. The dwarf added my name is Link and you may know my master who is Ping Lo. I shall not mention our names again so you do well to remember them. The consequences of falling foul of either one was a prospect no one wanted to contend. Link said "Know that betting is open now for the next five minutes to all and please remember we want you to be lucky tonight". Link drew back and sat on Ping Loe's knee.

Pedro had worked his way to the front of the crowd so he could see more clearly what was going on. A Mexican man came out of the throng and stated "I take up the challenge" as many more notes found their way to the heap on the table. The dwarf who was called Link said "we have a challenger; let it be so known that this man risks his life against all the wealth on this table. On his successful challenge his winnings here for all to see will be transported under Master Ping Loe's guard to whatever destination he desires.

Link shouted gentlemen you have one minute to place your final bets. Money flew onto the table from every direction. Anticipation hung in the air like a cloud. Finally, the time had come for the challenger they had waited for in a self-imposed silence that none would break. The big Mexican sat directly across from link who had now occupied his thrown at the last remaining part of the table where notes and gold did not take up the space. Link spread his small muscular legs to get a better balance. The large Mexican man tilted his head to the side as Link took the gun from Ping and curled a finger round the trigger. He said I take to the dangerous game but this time it is not cards that could befall me but only fate itself could challenge me. So bet as you will I intend to slay this demon who has slayed many

Ding Ding Ding! A bell sounded as Ping announced betting is now closed. The Mexican contender said "I am ready and I accept the challenge" and placed his head directly to the muzzle of the gun. Link pressed the gun so hard it made a red circle on the Mexicans temple. A hush went like a silent wave in the ocean around the punters. Link shouted to the gathered throng "without further ado I will discharge the pistol". The chamber revolved one step in the barrel and a bullet was loaded into waiting gun muzzle. A mechanical loud "Click" sound was heard as it moved.

The pistol ejected its deadly bullet from the guns loading barrel. Link shouted "misfire, all bets stand" as he cocked the pistol again moving the next chamber in line with its deadly cargo loaded as the punters shouted loudly "Misfire". Link waved his hands in a downward direction and the room fell silent once again. Those gamblers who had chosen round number two, felt more confident but it was to be rounds three, four and five were where the heaviest betting lay. Round Six was only for the foolhardy and the excessively rich.

Link again pressed the muzzle of the gun barrel home into the new contender's temple. Round One CLICK ... A smoking bullet again ejected as grey smoke rose from the muzzle. Link announced. The confidence of the gamblers had grown again.

Round Two CLICK ... a bullet had been fired but ejected and was a blank. It was found as more grey smoke rose from the muzzle. Link announced "gentlemen a blank has been found. We now move on to challenge four and I have much pleasure in announcing the Free round three after being handed the blank from it". The crowd erupted with shouts of round four echoed round the walls. Ping shouted over the din "gentlemen, gentlemen". The noise from the rabble began to calm down as Link readied himself for round FOUR, betting time for the round is now open for the next five minutes due to the it being blank round in round three All bets for round three still stand. Money poured on to the enormous pile of notes.

Link shouted gentlemen you have five minutes to place your final bets. Soon tickets from the betting window made the most direct way to the table. The crowd's anticipation hung in the air like a cloud. Finally, the time had come for the challenger to lower his head. The gamblers had waited for in a self-imposed silence that none would break. The big Mexican sat next to Link waiting.

Ding Ding Ding! A bell sounded the beginning of round four as Ping announced betting is now closed. The Mexican contender said "I am ready and I accept the challenge" and placed his head once more directly to the muzzle of the gun.

Link said "betting is now closed unless we have another contender" as the mechanical sound of the barrel moved on one place. CLICK ... the sound of the pistol was deafeningly made louder by the oppressing room walls. The crowd was heard to say after the shot Oh lord in unison. The Mexican fell stone dead on the stone floor. CLICK ... was the only sound heard as he hit the floor stone. He fell at the instant Link fired the fatal shot straight into the Mexicans brain. Some punters felt they had been cheated and made threats about getting their wagers returned to them. Out of nowhere stood six large well-armed men and their presence quickly silenced the throng.

Do we have another contender link demanded? Ping shouted across the crowded room. A man stepped forward. He was average weight, six feet two inches and solid muscle. Pedro stepped out of the crowd of gamblers to chants of good luck and slaps on the back.

Then the inevitable Click was the sound of the pistol was louder than it had been which greeted the crowd. But it was only the click of the hammer of the pistol hitting an empty chamber. The crowd roared with expectation. Click. Then wasting no time Link pulled the trigger yet again. Once more lady luck had filled an empty chamber. Link looked with a pretend anger and a forlorn expression as if all hope had been diminished while Ping gave an annoyed but sickly smile.

Link turned his head and winked at Ping. Then Link pressed the revolver to Pedro's temple as Link increased his pressure as if he was trying to bore a hole into his brain. Pedro waited patiently and silently without thinking about the fortune or the consequences of the challenge.

Anticipation was felt throughout the room once more. The clenched fists of the gamblers showed white knuckles and red patches where their blood was pooling on the back of their hands. Finally Link said is this the challenger who will take this fortune that is here sat waiting? Pedro simply said I accept the challenge! The amassed pile of gold, silver, notes and tickets now nearly covered the whole of the table. With gamblers there is no stopping and pausing for thought. The throng threw money, gold and silver onto the mountain of wealth as if it was of no value. Ping Loe thanked them and wished them every success without meaning or sincerity.

This time Link spun the barrel of the gun and pressed the muzzle into Pedro's temple. Link was excited to hear the inevitable Click. The sound of the pistol made a hollow tune as it fell on an empty chamber. The crowd roared with delight once again. CLICK ... the sound met with a sharp noise of the guns metal hammer hitting the bullet slightly to one side. and the crowd bellowed it's a blank.

For the Second round of the challenge Link wasted no time and pulled the trigger yet again. Ping shouted above the cacophonous din as two rounds and gone due to the bullet ejected. The gamblers seemed elated as the ejected. These regular challenge gamblers could not remember a time when such a thing had happened. Round Three is a pass due to mechanical failure. The fourth round is definitely for winners place your bets. After a short betting delay Link stated we now move onto round four. You all know the rules and good luck. The table didn't look like it could take any more weight. However, it did.

Then the inevitable Click ... as the pistol gave out the sickening sound of a backfire. Smoke filled the area. The throng of gamblers whooped, cheered and yelped loudly with shouts of Round five coming up. And so, it was decided by Ping that the round was passed. Ping passed link his own gun which was identical to the one which had misfired. Link looked confident and threw Ping a smile. The fifth bullet was ready to be fired and sat in its chamber as Link span the bullet drum. The crowd shouted together... that's Five as Pin called for calm. Meanwhile Link had slid the revolver drum under the table allowing no margin for error. The gun had to move to the logical next chamber on the next strike of the firing pin which meant that Pedro had no chance against a live bullet in a replacement gun. This time Link called for absolute silence, which was already in evidence throughout the room as so much was riding on it.

Click ... as the chamber ready to accept the fifth bullet inexplicably rolled over twice as the hammer once again hit an empty chamber. Link opened the revolver to allow him to see inside the chambers and sure enough the bullet had moved two cylinders instead of one. Link showed Pin the open chambers and threw him a look of complete disbelief. The noise of the crowd was excruciatingly loud. Pin stood and shouted the final round of betting will commence for the next five minutes. The gamblers searched every pocket they had and chatter filled the air with promises of payback as deals was struck between loans and repayments.

Thank you, gentlemen all betting is closed. The sixth and final round is due to begin. Absolute silence please as any noise will not be tolerated and your bet will be forfeit. Do I make myself clear Ping shouted. No one even wanted to make a sound to answer. Ping laid out an open right hand towards Link and said the master of ceremonies will now perform his duty. Link for the sixth and final time tortured the temple of Pedro with muzzle of the gun.

The sixth round clicked over ready to shoot. The hammer drew back waiting for its chance to strike. The determination on Links face made his cheeks begin to quiver. The sound of the shot was deafening as was the sound of lodged bullet did not make a move inside the barrel. There was a silence from the gamblers as the enormity of what had just happened began to sink in. Then slowly a victorious shout began to build in the crowd.

Pin Loe could not believe what just happened. How could it be so? Link turned to look at Pin Loe with disbelieving eyes. Pin Loe dismissed it with a wave of his hand. Link protested under his breath to Pin but he just stated "We have a winner". The crowd erupted and the din was loader than any that have ever been heard before. The outraged Link shouted please collect your winnings from the ticket window over there, pointing to the side of the room. The Que was noisy. Slowly the crowds made its way from the payout window and gradually it grew smaller until finally all payouts had been made.

Pedro stood alone still clapping at the gamblers good fortune, not realising his own. Finally Pin Loe said you have done well tonight. Pedro thanked him as he went on this has been one of our busiest nights for the last three years. Pedro interrupted and said I am pleased to have good fortune sir. Pin Loe pointed the flat of his hand at the enormous pile of gold bars, gold coins, large denomination notes and yet more gold coins nearly reaching the ceiling. It still had not been processed in Pedro's mind, he had never entered anything and he had never won anything in his life. Pedro looked at the beautiful cashier and bar maid as she asked Pedro if he would like a companion to ride in the coach with him. Pedro didn't know what to say so he just nodded his head and the pair left the room as the barmaid linked arms with him as if they were a courting couple. He was escorted out by the pretty barmaid

Chapter 4: Reminiscing

Now everyone had left Pin and Link made for the bar room. Link said, master, do you remember the time on the boat. I feel like reminiscing about the journey three years ago. Recalling the journey Link remembered the ship which brought them to Spain "The Carabao". It was an interesting voyage to be sure Link commented.

The cargo of the ordinary wooden sailing vessels had changed due to the Spanish governments ordering of an extra allowance for cargo's which ment Ships were now authorised to have increased cargos including mango de Manila, tamarind and rice. The "Carabao" was first brought into service in 1737 in Mexico, where no questions would be asked regarding birds for cockfighting, Chinese tea, tuba, coconut, textiles and fireworks for displays. It came to Mexico through the trans-Pacific Sea trade lines. All captains on the Pacific or Mediterranean trade routes must take on whatever brought profit for the ship's owners to keep the captains in a job.

Sailing day was today, the sun was overhead the "Carabao" saw hot sailors loading goods and welcoming passengers who embarked up a hurriedly laid wooden gangway. They were herded aboard by a ship worker he said welcome to the "Carabao". It was not a new ship and was one of the older sailing rigs. Having managed many miles on its journeys without disaster. It was a vessel which was painted often to make it look younger than its years. Onboard every type of cargo was taken including cocks for cockfighting, Chinese tea and textiles, fireworks for displays, tuba, coconut and wine all came onboard through the trans-Pacific trade route. A captain had to get whatever brought profit for the ships owners which was very difficult as every other ship's captain in port also wanted any cargo be it legal or otherwise, as long as it was paying cargo or goods that would make money. It was the lifeblood of the ship which would be captained until the next voyage when the owners would decide whether he was a profitable ship's captain or should be jettisoned like some much driftwood

The deck was now complete with forty-six migrants who were all escaping one captivity or another. A stout man of some fifty years looked through the wheel house window. There was a hush as men thought of the long journey and any danger they may face. Many desperate men just as they themselves shared the smallest amount of space and somehow, they knew this is where it all could end. If you ran into the wrong man or even if you did not, the laws of natural selection or the mood of the sea would be the judge here. Don't look for any help here one of the desperadoes thought, this is about the fittest men and is reliant on who has the brawn and the brains to survive.

A man walked out of the wheel house on the upper deck. He Said I am Captain Juan pepitaaso but you can call me Captain. Remember I run a tough ship and take no prisoners when it comes to breaking my rules of which there are only two. They are you do what I say, when I say it! Three large men appeared behind and at either side of him.

Link said I remember being sat on the deck rail. Me a Dwarf how dare I, Pin and Link laughed. Do you remember the large man that told me to get give him my place or he would stab me. Yes, I do Pin Said. Link thought back to when he grabbed the man's arm and was swung right round letting the him skid across the deck into deck wall at the other side. Link did not move as the large man stood straddling the dwarfs' legs at either side, still the dwarf did not move. The man reached down to the dwarf's chest.

Suddenly as fast as the eye could see the dwarf pushed away with his arms and slid between the man's legs. He twisted over and got a solid hold of the man's ankles and lifted them over his head tipping the man overboard. The rest of the men either laughed or jeered. As the captain nodded to the three sailors.

A tall thin man sat at the stern of the ship, pointed a curled finger towards the dwarf who thought what now but obliged him by going over. A half barrel sat next to the man who slapped it with the flat of his hand beckoning the dwarf to sit beside him which he did. The tall thin said and you are? My name is Link the dwarf told him. Let me introduce myself Link I am Pin Loe. The dwarf said pleased to meet you as Pin smiled saying I have a proposition for you. The two men discussed the proposition at length the thin man handed the dwarf a gold coin. To while away the journey Pin got a changing but small gathering as he played cards and would do magic tricks for a price which the dwarf held. Shouts of cheat could be heard as men left the gathering but beyond that no one did anything. A bell announcing the harbour disembarkation point rung. Pin and link were amongst the first to leave. And so it was that an association had been made. They made their way to a place called Veracruz and finally after a long walk camo to a place with an old sign which read "Veracruz old town" and they finally spotted a dilapidated saloon bar which had been put up for sale. Which Pin purchased in haste from the owner who was delighted to sell at a very low price as customers were few and profit was less.

Meanwhile Pin and Link continued reminiscing in the bar, thinking back on the circumstances they now found themselves in. They both drank heartily. Link began to think of his past as a Circus performer. He recollected one particular evening as Aleksandar who was a six-foot eight giant of a man. He wore a tiger outfit fastened over his shoulder. Aleksandar would bend iron bars and carryout other seemingly impossible feats of strength and thrilled audiences nightly. Link was a dwarf strongman and the crowds loved him so out he strode from behind the red curtain at the rear of the ring. Link though small of stature was a muscle-bound dwarf, just a shade under four feet. The crowd would hoot and go wild. Link stood behind Aleksandar and then would move to the left at the side of him, whilst Aleksandar who looked down at Link disapprovingly. Link then moved to the right of Aleksandar who once again gave a stare looking at his feet and the released a grunt which was heard throughout the main even tent. Aleksandar glanced left and right. As Aleksandar reached and he grabbed Link and threw Link over his shoulder and then threw him down to the sandy floor. Link landed on his rear and slowed up as he came to rest in the sand. The audience booed and jeered seeing the giant taking his annoyance out on the dwarf. The Ringmaster asked would you like to see the Hungarian giant Aleksandar up close. A murmur went around the tent as apprehension flew through parents. The ringmaster announced "Ladies, Gentlemen and Children telling them that the wooden painted boxes which surrounded the main tent just in front of the audience. This is a circular track for you to be able to see Aleksandar closer than any audience has ever seen him.

The ringmaster shouted "Then without further Ado, I give you Aleksandar the Hungarian giant". Aleksandar then made his way round the inner ring with his huge arms extended to either side of him and his fingers were splayed as if he was about to catch a member of the audience. Children, some crying, some were wrapped in their mothers' arms hoping Aleksandar would move on. As he was reaching towards the end of the encircled boxes Link appeared from the curtain at the rear and stood outside of the boxes with a large stick. Just as Aleksandar got to the last three boxes. The crowd pointed and shouted with glee as children laughed. Aleksandar looked puzzled at the audience as Link struck with his stick on the back of Aleksandar. Parents and children laughed so loud it could be heard outside the circus. Aleksandar rubbed his back as Link challenged him to a strength contest. Aleksandar immediately agreed and four extra performers rolled a large iron bar onto the centre of the ring. The four performers struggled to lift the iron bar and kept it only inches from the sand and then dropping it into the floor. They kept looking solid iron bar with its black weights on either end with a quarter of a ton written on them in large white lettering. Aleksandar pulled a bold face and laughed at his dwarf opponent as he covered his hands with white chalk powder to help his grip. Aleksandar let out an animal roar from his six-foot eight-inch frame as an ooh rippled through the crowd as Aleksandar bent his knees and then wrapped his hands around the steel bar. Aleksandar let out a mighty noise showing his maximum effort, however the bar sat stubbornly in the sand. The second attempt appeared to drain Aleksandar even more. After a final attempt Aleksandar kicked the sand in disgust. The ringmaster announced and now for our second contender Link the worlds dwarf strongman. The crowd clapped so loud the canvas sides of the main ring saw waves of sound bouncing off them. Link looked determined and focused as his hands slid into the chalk bowl and his arms went out in front of him as he locked his fingers with his palms facing outward.

Silence fell throughout the tent as Aleksandar stood to one side and looked on with a half-smile. Link took two paces and surveyed the iron bar with the weights that had defeated Aleksandar. Pulling a grimace on his face he bent down and grabbed the bar but just as quickly let go. The weighted bar looked as if it had no intention of being raised. Link then took a second stance to grab the bar, however once again it stubbornly sat as it had before when Aleksandar had tried to lift it without success. Link said I do this not to beat Aleksandar but I do this for you my audience and you alone. Women were shouting please don't hurt yourself Link if it is too heavy stop. Link clapped his shoulders as if warming himself up for the momentous task that he must now take on. Finally, he gave a loud hand clap Clouds of smoke swirling in the air from the white chalk powder to help his grip, then dived onto the bar with both hands and pulled the bar up to his chest as the crowd erupted into shrieks, shouts, claps and encouragement. Link did not disappoint them but raised the bar still higher. The bar sat level above Links head as the audience was both united and elated emitting an even louder shout.

In the bar area Pin said Well tonight was unfortunate I thought what is your opinion. Link agreed and nodded his head as Pin took two bottles from the shelf behind the bar and began pouring.

Chapter 5: The Hotel

Pin pointed at the beautiful cashier and bar maid asked Pedro if he would like a companion to ride in the coach with him. Pedro didn't know what to say so he just nodded his head and the pair left the room as the barmaid linked arms with him as if they were a courting couple.

Seven large chests were brought into the room by four men. They opened the chests which stood next to the very large table and they filled them one by one and padlocked each chest lid. The men stood arms folded awaiting instructions from Pin. Pin congratulated Pedro on his amazing achievement and told him that he would be taken to the local Hotel by Pins own carriage. Once there he would have the best room in the hotel for as long as he wished to stay. Pedro hardly knew what to say his mind was spinning with ten thousand thoughts at once. Pin could see Pedro was disorientated and just said in croaky voice thank you.

Pedro and the girl from the bar climbed into the carriage and the coachman waited for the last chest to be secured he then set off at a fast pace and handled the carriage expertly swinging first left then right at speed. The bar girl gripped Pedro's arm and nuzzled her face into his shoulder.

The coach drew to a stop at the steps of the hotel. and its two passengers alighted to the main door of the Hotel Talavera. They were met at the front desk by a tall thin man wearing horn rimmed spectacles. He swivelled a big registration book round. Pedro had no inkling of what it meant or what he was supposed to do with it as the thin man passed a quill pen to Pedro who just looked at it as if he was studying a work of art.

Realising his predicament the bar girl asked if she may fill in the details needed to register for Pedro and he gratefully agreed. The pair of them the climbed the stairs and the girl produced a key and stated this is your room as she opened the door.

Pedro had never seen anything like it and was in awe of its splendour. A large wooden neatly carved bed lay against the far wall. Pictures adorned the walls and solid framed mirror hung near the bay window with fresh flowers in a fancy vase scented the room just below the mirror.

The girl asked if everything was satisfactory and Pedro could do no more than nod. With that the girl smiling disappeared back through the door. Pedro sat on the bed and removed his boots. He then lay on the great fluffy pillow staring up the chandelier which glinted and sparkled from every facet.

For some time, he sat on the bed trying to make sense of the day's events when a knock came at the door. Surprised he got up and opened it to see his companion who had shared the coach with him. The girl stood there holding a tray with Brandy, Rum and whiskey and adorned with sandwiches of every type. Pedro held the room door open and as she the carried the tray to a gold inlaid mahogany table. Pedro closed the door and said please I thank you for your kindness. He stood quite still famished with hunger and thirst but the sight of the silver tray simply terrified him as he had never encountered the like of this lavishness. He went back to sitting on the bed.

The girl said it is only room service do not concern yourself, now eat drink and if you would like more of anything you only have to ask. She plumped herself on the bed next to him saying now what shall we have first. She jumped to her feet and snapped the silver tray up slotting it between them.

Pedro had never imagined a grand buffet like it and he didn't know quite what to reach for. The girl dug in and encouraged him to try everything feeding some Caviar toast and he seemed to like it even though he had never tasted it before. Munching away on the toast Pedro asked what sort of farms harvest this. The girl laughed loudly and then said I am sorry; I did not mean to laugh. Pedro said to her it's alright not knowing what had caused the humour. Finally, the girl repeated how sorry she was and said in a lowered voice said it does not come from a farm, the Beluga Caviar comes from the sea.

Pedro's response was not one of indignation but rather it was of resignation from his ignorance. But he really did not need to feel that as he was a farm boy who had had little or no education and his schooling had been driving a plough sheer for the livelihood of the farm for his father, mother and Pedro accepted it like the sunrise in the morning.

He resigned himself to the fact he would understand the ways of this new life. The girl saw him deep in thought next to her on the bed and finally interrupted them, Great isn't it I'm loving the food, are you? I can have more or different food brought up she continued depending on whatever your taste may be. Pedro said everything has been wonderful. But all he really wanted was to sleep as it had been such a busy day. Then quite without discussion he "said no more food for me however I would love a drink to wash it down. The girls eyed lit up and she immediately crossed the room opened the door and called for the tray of food to be taken away This was replaced with a new tray of the best liquor. And so it was, the two of the seemed to agree on the Courvoisier Napoleon Brandy. Round thick Havana cigars also abounded on the silver tray. Sometime later Pedro fell asleep on the bed.

It was early in the morning and Pedro was awakened from his forced slumber by a heaving sound and some bumping and banging. Startled Pedro looked across the room to the window alcove where seven large heavy chests now filled the space. One of the big surly men whom he recognised as loading the chests on the rear of the coach which had brought him to the hotel said are they alright here sir. Pedro half asleep said that's good and just wanted him to go so he could forget his exhaustion and fall back into dream about the milkmaid delivering to a farm.

Seven large chests were brought into the room by four large men. They opened the chests which stood next to the very large table and they filled them one by one and padlocked each chest lid. The men stood arms folded awaiting instructions. Pin congratulated Pedro on his amazing achievement and told him that he would be taken to the local hotel by Pins own carriage. Once there he would have the best room in the hotel for as long as he wished to stay. Pedro hardly knew what to say his mind was spinning with ten thousand thoughts at once. Pin could see Pedro was disorientated as stated thank you in a croaky tone.

The following morning Rose woke up with a blinding headache the like of which she had never known. It was accompanied by a dry mouth and what felt like a procession of drums taking residence in the centre of her skull. She rolled out of bed and made it as far as the fourth step on the stairs and beckoned the hotel manager to bring Dr Olivers no 1. snake oil. No sooner than she had formed the words than the manager at speed passed her as she caught hold of his jacket. She said in the loudest Croke that would come, it's for me. The manager who had seen her attempt the stairs the previous evening knew full well who it was for as he handed her the square bottle and replied very good madam.

Rose sat on her bed and saw the label which read Dr Olivers No. 1 snake oil which can fix anything from a toothache to a bad stomach. On the back it read. for sickness take one cupful. for a medical problem take two cupful's and if you believe you may be dying take three cupful's. If symptoms persist you need to take Dr Olivers snake oil No. 1 each and every day.

Rose was way past caring and took a cupful never knowing what was in it. Sometime later she recovered from her stupor when the throbbing headache had reduced but not gone. She went to the bathroom mirror in her room which was over the sink and tried to wash away her sins from the night before. After a half hour or so looking more presentable to sit in company Rose left her room and made the stairs in the most ladylike way she knew how. As she reached the foyer the manager pointed at the morning room. Rose sat opposite from Pedro and simply greeted him with a good morning.

Chapter 6: The Day Trip

Good morning, Rose Pedro replied. What time did you go to your bed. Rose's cheeks coloured somewhat and proclaimed oh not late. Are you feeling well this day Pedro asked. yes, I am I just need my breakfast Rose said with a wry smile as Pedro commented me too. I'm sorry Rose questioned. Have you been waiting long? Pedro wishing to save her any embarrassment stated no, not very.

Duly Breakfast arrived and was finished before they knew it. Pedro announced that today was to be a day of surprises. Rose asked timidly what is it. She made some excuse about its importance as she must know what wear. Pedro laughed and said you look fine as you are.

The hotel manager suddenly arrived and told him Sir the coach is awaiting you. Pedro was not pleased by the interruption and said tell him to wait until we are ready. We will be along shortly. The hotel manager left the morning room with a very good sir.

Pedro and Rose left and climbed into the coach. Pedro pointed out of the window with his newly acquired and expensive cane. The coach driver set off at pace and entered a long and slightly winding road. The two were buffeted around inside the coach but they both endured it with word or complaint.

They arrived at the fishing village of Cudillero a picturesque fishing port. The views were simply breathtaking; a calm blue sea, the harbor walls fortified to signify days now passed, the cobbled streets leading to the main shopping street in Cudillero. The style of the church in front of them was gothic and dated back to the sixteenth century and housed many baroque paintings Rose said what are we here to see. Pedro simply replied we are here to shop.

The town seemed somewhat deserted compared to what Pedro had in his mind of how a fishing port should be, bustling streets filled with a throng of buyers who wanted to buy the latest catches. The driver opened the carriage door on Rose's side first the moved around to Pedro's side with some speed and dexterity. Pedro Thanked him but didn't have any money to offer in the form of a tip. Thank you, Sir announced the coach driver, and to save any embarrassment he continued it is my pleasure and duty to serve so no thanks or payment is required or necessary.

With That Pedro walked around the other side of the carriage to meet Rose who linked arms with him immediately. The walkway in front of the shops was made of wooden boards to lift them above the mud which occasionally crossed the street like a path to sodden shoe and boot heaven.

The pair of them stayed on the left side of the mud road even when it became dry. Pedro saw a shop window which made him stop. He looked at a Stetson hat and another beside it which had a Panama hat with a curve at the front where the two rims of the hat met from the sides. Pedro entered the shop and took both hats inquiring if the shopkeeper had the hats in his size. Indeed, we do sir as we have stock in most of the required sizes. Do you have a Stetson which is made of leather and has a band around its base. Indeed, we do sir however I do not have the space to show all our stock in the window you will understand. Rose interjected and of course what suits do have. Anything Madam wishes the store attendant said... then added ... are you with the monsieur. Pedro shut him down quite abruptly and said yes, she is do you have a problem with that! The store attendant bent low and said no, please know if I have offended in any way the problem is all mine and I beg forgiveness.

Suddenly a realisation came to Pedro that his wealth even though he did not know what that maybe was being wielded like a sword by the girl. He wondered did he have enough to pay for all the clothes he wanted to buy. What Pedro did not know was that while he had been trying on hats Rose was busy with attendant and she was telling him rather than explaining that the store would be very wealthy very quickly. Rose gave the man the address of the hotel. The store clerk admitted they could send a telegram from the local mail office. Rose said this is likely to be a large order... can you handle that? The store clerk said of course madam. She then told him she wanted twelve suits in blue and green and everyday suits of the latest cuts all in his size. Rose then demanded twenty-four shirts to match the suits and they must be the top quality or she would reject the entire order at the hotel.

Meanwhile Pedro who had heard little of any conversations asked about belts to which the storekeeper replied. I am sorry sir the display items are all we carry. Not what I require Pedro replied as the attendant looked down at his boots as thought had the answer.

They then crossed the street without assault from the mud as Pedro spotted the belt shop Cording's Belts The both continued on the other side of the street and entered the belt shop. He said do you have a range of belts in my size as Rose produced a pair of his trousers from under her arm. Pedro looked pleasantly surprised as he looked over the most suitable belts. The man behind the counter told him we can have any belt lengthened or shortened as per Sirs requirement.

Rose gave the store manager details of payment and then she left the store and caught up with Pedro. on the other side of the street Pedro saw a sign pronouncing belts, belts, belts and he made a beeline for the shop. Rose saw his interest and the two of them entered glancing at the goods that had been proudly displayed in the shop window. Pedro set to work looking through rack after rack of belts. He chose six of them and Rose explained where they were to be delivered and who to contact for payment.

Nearly four hours later both of them were all shopped out which the coach driver had anticipated and drew alongside them as he heard a mutter of oh thank the Lord as they entered the coach.

The coach duly drove off and reached the hotel in double quick time. Rose told the driver to wait as she would be coming out shortly. In the hotel Pedro said I am going to my room and thank you for your help today. Less than five minutes had passed and Pedro lay sound asleep on his big comfortable bed. While Rose slipped out of the hotel and re-entered the coach.

Without a word passing their lips the driver knew where to take Rose. They soon pulled up at the bar. Pin sat waiting at a table. So where have you been he questioned. Oh, shopping she said nonchalantly. Did you buy anything nice Pin asked. Nothing for me she told him. But we bought half the goods in Marten town. Pin suddenly became agitated and jumped to his feet. He began to march up and down with zeal. Link stopped swinging his legs which dangled as he sat on the bar. It's not enough the he takes seven chests of my treasure but now he humiliates me further with this outrage. Pins face was red with anger as his blood pressure flooded his cheeks.

Oh, I am sorry Pin, Rose said as she placed a hand on his back trying to calm him down. Pin brushed her hand away booming loudly by proclaiming don't touch me. Just then a whiskey bottle exploded on the shelf next to the mirror on the bar and shattered into pieces on the floor. Pin could see the shock on Links face and said oh the heat makes them do that each year. Link was satisfied with the explanation Pin had given but he did not believe it as he had seen Pin Glaring at the Whiskey bottle at the exact moment it had exploded.

Rose was a very intelligent girl and she knew she must choose her next words carefully. What would you like me to do Pin, she asked knowing what his answer would be. Pin swivelled round with military precision. Get close to him he said. Become his stave, Link looked puzzled as Pin directed his gaze toward him explaining to Link it's a staff, a stick for support, something to lean on it's called a stave. Oh, link said and immediately fell silent. Rose commented I can do that. He must not know or suspect anything Pin went on. This is your task. You do this for me and all will be well with your life but you disobey me and the consequences are too horrible to even think about. Rose was taken aback but knew the way to Pins dark heart. I will do as I have always done, she said. Pin concluded she had been well trained and as if she read his very thoughts smiled and replied well, I had a great teacher. Pin was satisfied and did not believe she had created the performance of her life even thought that was what was at stake. Right, he said go back and remember what we have spoken of this day as it would be a great shame to lose you Rose. She said I must quickly discuss payment with you as delivery of goods are to go to the hotel and I gave your name as guarantor. Pin stated you know my terms one quarter of the face spending value. Rose knew his fee had always been one tenth however she erred on the side of caution agreeing to the fee. If I am asked, what do you want me to say it is for. Is it likely you will be asked Pin inquired. I don't know Rose said. Pin told her it is for my considerable influence. Oh, she said of course but now I must be getting back.

Returning to the Hotel Rose soon sat in the hotel bar contemplating Pins words and knew full well what they meant. Pin Loe was a killer and it gave him pleasure and so far, there was no earthly force that had changed that. He was an agent of the dark forces if ever she had known one. Which she had not. This uncomfortable thought played on her mind until late in the night when strong drink took over. Rose was fearful and thought what am I to do? Then when her final piece of sobriety that had not succumbed to the torrent of drink, she had a fleeting thought, I need to do Pins bidding be it right wrong or indifferent. Tomorrow morning, all her musings would be washed away in the brandy river which she had drunk this night. She needed sleep and aimed roughly in the direction of it.

Chapter 7: Castle Alverez

After breakfast the coach driver announced their journey was waiting for them whenever they were ready to go. Pedro left the table first and Rose followed and they walked with a forthright step towards the waiting coach which once they were aboard left at speed.

The coach driver announced their arrival at Castle Alverez. Pedro stepped out first. and walked with determination towards a large iron clad dark oak front door. He tugged on a thick iron bell pull. There was a short wait before the door was opened.

A tall thin man wearing circular horn-rimmed spectacles said. Welcome, welcome, welcome in an upper-class English tone. They were shown into a lavish sitting room and the suns shadow appeared to break the room into one bright and one dark half. They were beckoned to join the tall thin man on a comfortable couch. Pedro waved his hand in Roses direction and told her to look around with which she withdrew from the room. The thin tall man stated my name is Charles Fortesque and asked to what do I owe your visit. Is it business or pleasure. Pedro commented, down to business I am Pedro and Rose is the one inspecting your castle. Which I may purchase from you.

Pedro said, tell me about yourself Charles. Oh, I see the bespectacled man said. I am English Charles went on in an authoritative voice. Charles said he had been the school governor at saint Andrew's boys' college in Edinburgh for seven years before he went on to explain the job had become mundane and he needed a change of scenery so he opted to take up a post in London as the Head Bursar at St Thomas' private academy until one day he opened an invitation from a man called Carlos Alvarez who resided in Spain. I accepted an offer and came Spain. I should point out the benefits of working in this castle and for my employer. Well, it just seemed too good to pass up on. That was five years ago. The owner of this castle is Signor Alvarez and he is a good employer. All my food and lodgings were found each month and all I had to do was to buttle. Pedro looked with astonishment not because of the position Charles held but because he had never come across the word in his life and knew not what it referred to. Charles saw the confusion lines on Pedro's forehead and continued as you are already aware my job was to help Mr Alvarez' every requirement to be a butler of standing. Pedro sat forward as his interest peaked in Charles. In answer to your question about my purpose visiting you, I wish to speak to Mr Alvarez, is he upstairs Charles. Charles sighed and said no sir he is not.

As regards to the kind of man he is, Señor Alverez is a wealthy tortured soul, he is driven by his Catholic religion, gambling and his insatiable lust for wealth. He is a very solitary man who keeps his own council. His intentions and opinions are his own and it as part of his mystique and secrecy. I am his butler, his house keeper and his confidante. Charles was a very discreet man but knew today was an important day in the life of the castle and he must not lose a client because he would not divulge Señor Alverez's characteristics. Alverez had searched for the type of man Charles was. Generally, Señor Alverez's belief was no gossip, no speculation and very little conversation other than the weather and the view. So little was gleaned from Señor Alverez in the five years that had passed. Charles was more than a butler, he was in Señor Alverez' eyes a man servant who was there to take care of his every comfort. Alverez's gambling had gotten to the stage where he was obliged to ask for larger and larger sums from his family's estate. Charles had surmised in his mind that Señor Alverez would be grateful to

Charles for even the notion of a sale, which his employer had discussed recently that if such an opportunity arose, he should look at it seriously. Señor Alverez's family had hinted their wine vineyards were having a particularly good year and profits had been soaring. What price do you propose to offer for the castle Charles asked. Just then Rose came in and her excellent hearing coupled with her business acumen forced her to interrupt. I remember hearing that when Mr Alvarez purchased the castle it was sold for around two million Peseta' isn't that so Rose said as she directed a piercing gaze at Charles. However, she continued due to the lack of upkeep and the amount of work needed to restore it to its former glory. I would have thought in today's market with a lack of buyers with the funds available to purchase such a property, its condition and the state of Spain's economic circumstances that the not inconsiderable sum of half a million would be more than sufficient to purchase it.

He was taken aback by Rose' forthright style and boldness. Charles looked up from under his glasses at Pedro questioning brow. Is Sir in agreement with the lady's evaluation of the property? Pedro though a mere farm hand in his earlier life was no fool and told Charles, Rose is my right-hand adviser in all things, if she believes that is what should be offered then that is the offer. Charles took this as a yes and questioned so Sir wishes to take this as a formal offer for the castle. Pedro said yes indeed and without delay. If Sir will excuse me, I will be back shortly. With that Charles left the room and headed for the study. Picking up the telephone he was shortly connected and said Mr Alvarez.

Charles answered lowering his voice in the study and explained that he had finally had an offer on the Castle. That would mean there would be little need to ask your family for money for a few years. The two men chatted at length. Mr Alvarez had fallen on hard times; he told Charles and was greatly in need of funds. Charles suspected this was the case before he had even lifted the telephone receiver. Well Sir no other offers have been received these past five years. What would you like me to tell them sir. Tell them yes of course Alverez shouted. Very good Sir it shall be done. The whole transaction will be completed by tomorrow afternoon Sir. With that Alvarez said always good to speak to you Charles. Make sure payment is in the bank by no later than two O' Clock tomorrow. Charles said yes Sir before replacing the receiver knowing Señor Alverez accepted the offer without hesitation whilst he must be imagining alleviating the local gambling establishment of funds where he was staying as a resident.

Pedro was still staring out of the window down the mountain road when Charles returned. Is he coming here Charles Pedro asked when he returned to the room. Alas no Sir he is away somewhere on one of his trips. I am sorry sir he has given me no date when he will return. However, the good news is your offer has been accepted. Stunned Pedro immediately asked will he not wish to meet me? Charles said oh that will not be necessary once the bank has accepted payment. Thinking of changing the subject, Charles eyes looked toward the curved roof above them and at the life size Solid wood crucifix that hung from gold chains suspended more than thirty feet in the air. Those dots you see around the crucifix which shine so brightly are all genuine silver. Tell me more Pedro said. As you now know Sinure Alvarez is a very religious man. And before he became the mayor of the town below us, the crucifix was his most proud achievement. As he believed he had pleased the Lord by his efforts to display him on high. That and the central glass dome which nestled on the top floor was indeed the crowning glory of the castle. Pedro Eyed the statue in amazement wondering why he had never seen anything in a church to match its magnificence. Charles read his face and said it was made by a master craftsman in Italy. The wood from which it is carved is Rosewood and is imported directly from Honduras. It was hanging here when I came five years ago and became as much part of the castle as we who were living in it.

Charles re-entered the sitting room where he found Rose and Pedro deep in discussion. My apologies for the lengthy conversation with Mr Alvarez he said. However, I bring good news your offer is accepted at the earlier agreed amount. Pedro was delighted and his face did not try to hide it. Pedro announced tomorrow is going to be a very full day, therefore I will stay here this evening. Charles nodded and said delighted to have you both as my guests. Your rooms are made up and will accommodate you whenever you are ready. Rose questioned him she said "your guests". Yes, madam nothing more than a figure of speech it is purely that you will not officially own the castle until the clock strikes two tomorrow afternoon. Thats fine Pedro said. Charles you will need to set aside about two hours in the morning when I wish to speak to you. Mortal dread filled Charles' heart as he thought he knew what the conversation would entail. Very good sir he replied.

Alas Charles added. I do not say this lightly as I have said he is a fine man Señor Alverez had gone from the castle leaving a hand written note on the dining table stating he would contact me in due course when he had become settled and he thanked me for my service and hoped I would find a suitable post, then signed it Señor Alvarez your friend.

Did he have any vices? Well sir his only vice was gambling and he would climb in his carriage and disappear for days at a time. Did he drink Pedro asked. Indeed, he did not sir. I know because I looked after his books. Books Pedro inquired. Ah sorry sir I refer to business account ledgers. This duly led to the evening I visited him in his study and with great sadness I told him the money was largely depleted. Pedro thought what terrible predicament to befall him. It came to him as a great shock. Later that evening Señor Alverez's asked me what have you ever done for me over these years, as if I was soley to blame. Oh well it was good while it lasted hey. Charles began thinking selfishly at first. Thinking of his own position and trusted relationship, whilst visioning the life had built up with the grand the roof over his head which may be removed by who moved in. He thought about his situation and where he would move to and what would become of him. Charles thoughts were spinning at dizzying speed. He thought about what might become of him, should he try work up a fair to return to England, should he try and locate the cheapest boarding house in the area. Then an uncomfortable yet likely thought struck him. What if they were in a relationship. Would they ask him to leave immediately to have privacy and the castle to themselves.

Pedro asked the question people had wondered down the years, tell me Charles how did Mr Alvarez come into his wealth. Charles gave a cough and replied... old family money Sir. His family own a large estate with vineyards to the north somewhere. I never really did know its location except to say a telegram would arrive from A bank called Banco Hispano when Mr Alvarez needed to fill the coffers.

However, one month later Señor Alverez was taken ill with Cholera. The papers stated it was an epidemic and nothing more could be done at the time apart from burning the corpse to stop the spread of the decease. The papers said Señor Alverez had been taken with a short illness lasting only a few weeks. One of Spain's most notable doctors Jose Rizal who had qualified with exceptional results at the Universidad De Central Madrid in 1888 where he completed his studies before moving to the University of Santo Tomas to study disease.

Señor Alverez's body had been disposed of by the state. After examining the body his death was recorded as death by disease and in the margin the date and Cholera had been written, signed at the bottom was the signature of Dr Jose Rizal. The Corpse was buried and he was no more. The modern Spanish Civil Registry system was created in 1870 during the reign of King Amadeo I, who imported the idea of a non-ecclesiastical registration of deaths from his native Italy; the law came into effect on 1 January 1871, and began by only recording births, marriages and deaths (not including stillbirths or children who died within the first twenty-four hours after birth). The funeral was attended only by paid mourners. Charles was devastated by the news.

Charles sat quietly and contemplated the thought of how he had ended up in a Spanish Castle and the incident which had led to this. Charles was, determined, celibate and driven to achieve whatever he did. He had been at St Andrews School for Boys when the annual fencing competition came round and with only one day to go, he was matched against the school's best boy who excelled at fencing, his name was James McMasters. Charles knew this was going to be a tough match McMasters was in a class of his own and Charles knew it. Let the bout begin he called in the final preliminary. The sword play was outstanding from both master and pupil. Parry after parry thrust after thrust then a single moment and McMasters was ahead on points, one more and he had beaten the master who would not be allowed to compete tomorrow. Charles felt the dual was slipping away from him, then a chance as McMasters turned sideways to make himself a smaller target. Charles lunged having removed the dagger tip of his sword behind his back he dropped it on the floor, thrusting the deadly blade down into McMasters armpit. McMasters fell to the fighting mat. The blade had cut across his heart and James McMasters was dead as he hit the floor.

The school governors met the following day and had a private meeting about what was to be done with respect to this incident. Mcnern one of the housemasters said what about our reputation, do you think those of influence will allow their children to be educated here? Pogget replied but he is a great master of some long standing with an exemplary record. Parkman another of the housemasters commented until now. Gateland banged his gavel on the table and said place your vote in the envelope provided and pass it to me. Rising from his chair Gateland shuffled the envelopes into a pack and said until two O' clock this afternoon gentlemen.

Duly two O'clock arrived and they all came into the committee room. Charles was the last to follow as they all got seated. Charles Fortesque this is not a court of law but is a disciplinary hearing. We have parents wishing to take their sons out of the school, we have a minister asking for an update the moment this meeting is over. Mr Fortesque what do you have to say for yourself? Charles said the only thing he could. It was an accident pure and simple. Gateland raised his eyebrows as heavy frown lines mixed with a look of distain on his face. Gateland told him there was nothing "pure" or "simple" in this incident. It has left one tragic death, disastrous consequences for the family and an uncertain future for the school. Charles lowered his head saying I don't know how it happened the safety tip must have fallen on the floor and due to it being behind me I lunged without knowing. Seems reasonable to me Pogget said. Gateland said in an annoyed voice "Be Quiet" Pogget or I will have you removed from the room. So Gateland continued you are our fencing champion of the past seven years and yet was unable to best a schoolboy without injury to say nothing of killing him. Charles argued none of you understand, it was an accident.

Gateland Opened the voting envelopes and laid them out in front of him. Gentleman the question was should Charles Fortesque remain in post or be removed. The results are unanimous four to one. Charles Fortesque you are forthwith removed from your post and you may not step on these school grounds again.

Sighs of relief went around the table as one low voice said thank God that's over. They all rose from their chairs and streamed out of the room.

Since a boy all Pogget had wanted was to satisfy his love of knowledge. Education allowed him to read every book in his father's library. He was from an early age destined for Oxbridge. First gaining a higher Degree in Oxford then later attending Cambridge to become a student of note. He had garnished many awards from both universities. They just cluttered a small cabinet in his room but went unnoticed by Pogget as he thought of them as insignificant prizes rather than acknowledgements for outstanding achievement. Since he was a boy at school, he had been friendless but his solitary nature made his outlook one of apathy Pog didn't care what the other children thought or said. His enthusiasm was for books, academic study and a curiosity which drove him to be better in each new subject he studied. Professor Pogget was a singular man of habit and filled with curiosity for the world in which he lived. His friends of which he had only one, called him Pog.

Charles Fortesque Walked up to Professor Pogget's front door and knocked loudly. Pogget Sat reading and drinking a last strong whisky. He rose slowly thinking who could it be as he had so few visitors. Charles greeted him with a warm smile and bottle of the best whiskey. Good evening Pog he said and was greeted with a hello Charles what lovely surprise as he eyed the bottle of whisky. Come in Charles Pog said and they both sat down in the reading room. Charles passed him the whiskey and said Professor Poggety, I will come straight to the point. I thank you for how you tried to help me today I am truly most grateful. Poggety said I wish I could have done more but you know how it is when the clan meets. Charles said think nothing of it, you did your best in an impossible situation and again my sincere thanks go to you.

I have visited you this evening because I need a Favor that only you can do. Well, what is it Professor Pogget said. Charles went on to tell him he had seen an opening for a butler in The Times newspaper jobs offered section. Pog said oh how wonderful you must apply and give it your best. What I need Pog is a benefactor. Pog said do you need money Charles. No no nothing like that Pog what I need is a friend who can reference me in a good light which would stand out from the page and make my future employer want to see me. Oh, is that all dear boy Pog said. Not exactly it needs to be on St Andrews School headed paper, headed up with your full qualifications and best authority. And written in such a way as only you Professor Poggety can write. It shall be done Pog stated. Charles said the vacancy Pog is actually in Spain. Taken aback Pog said so I shall not be seeing you again my dear friend. Charles remarked if you are successful in your task let us, just say not for a while anyway. Well, Pog declared its best foot forward and I will do everything possible to secure the post. The two men rose and shook hands whilst clapping each other on the back. A tearful Pog showed Charles to the door and wished him again every success for the future.

The very next day Pog laid out on his desk a very ornate Spanish dictionary with gold lettering on the front. He began by stating that his acquaintance with Charles went back some eleven years and, in that time, he could not recall a single incident that was not to Charles credit. He further went on to describe his qualities as trustworthy, reliable, discreet, skilful, loyal and honest. Pog said in his letter that Charles Fortesque comes to you Señor Alverez with my personal recommendation and that he will be both sorely missed and difficult to replace. It is with our regret that he has seen your vacancy and that he has his mind set as to how he may enhance your life by his service.

Barely two weeks past when a postman carrying a telegram arrived at Charles door. Charles took the telegram and gave him all the change in his pocket to the post man. He sat at the kitchen table and slowly opened the telegram. It read congratulations you have been successful and begin your duty as my new butler on the twenty seventh of this month. Please let me know forthwith if you intend to accept this role. I have provided a ticket for your complete travel to my home. All expenditures have been included for your ease.

Charles was more than delighted and would see Professor Pogget this evening and share his good news after he had purchased a bottle of the very best malt whisky, he could find to thank Pog for his efforts.

Charles' thoughts were broken the next morning as halfway down the hill outside castle the Church clock stuck five O' clock. Charles had had a fitful sleep in the chair until his brain just stopped racing as tiredness took over the reins. Charles was up and working on breakfast in the kitchen when the racing thoughts re-entered his mind. He found it difficult to concentrate on the breakfast he was making and tried very hard to dismiss them but he had very little success. The church clock rang announcing that it was now ten O' clock precisely.

Rose came down early and found Charles in his kitchen preparing breakfast. Pedro descended the stairs and made for the sitting room where Rose was sat waiting. Good morning, Rose did you sleep well he said. Yes, thank you Pedro I slept wonderfully and you Rose inquired. Me too. yesterday's business must have taken its toll for I cannot remember my head hitting the Pillow. Rose smiled. Just then Charles appeared with a pencil and a small notepad. What can I get you both this fine morning? Pedro and Rose gave him their order and sat silently throughout breakfast. Charles noticed the lack of conversation and wondered if it might be the tension of what they later had to tell him. He knew he was over thinking things but seemed unable to break the spell.

Rose and Charles talked for over an hour and they showed a mutual respect. They just naturally seemed to hit it off. Charles felt more comfortable in Rose's presence now. When Breakfast was over Pedro said which is the most suitable room for us all to a talk. Charles replied the Study sir. Pedro Said then we will all adjourn to the study. Once in the study Pedro sat behind the big desk and ordered them to be seated in the two smaller chairs in front of the desk. Well now I have to tell you "Pedro hardy believed it was him speaking" you are hopefully going to be my right-hand man so to speak, if you accept my proposal, Rose. Smiling he continued, Charles you will be my assistant. Charles if you also accept my proposal, Do I make myself clear he asked as confusion reigned as the two of them looked incredulously at each other. I realize this may come as a shock to you, however I should tell you that Charles you continue to stay on in the roll I have described. Your salary is up to you and guaranteed by me. Rose you are my business adviser and as such your salary will be whatever you think is fair. Your answers please Pedro said?

After a short-glazed glance at each other Rose and Charles agreed unanimously. Right Pedro commented. Charles you are to be my educator amongst many other duties. Yes, sir Charles said with some glee. Rose you are to be my financial business partner. Rose nodded her head vigorously. Pedro seemed quite pleased with himself at being able to deliver his speech. Very well then, he said. The work starts now. Rose you look over the books to which she nodded and Charles you will order a carriage from wherever. Charles looked sheepish but continued Sir if I may be so bold. May I make a suggestion. Yes, indeed Charles, that is you job. Well Sir if I hire the carriage from each week, it may make more sense to own it if funds allow. Pedro looked deeply into the desk as though the answer was written there. Rose broke their thoughts and said Yes that makes sense. Pedro advised Charles as if it had been his idea and said I thank you all. Charles, will you get advice from Rose and buy the carriage we arrived in. Oh, and Charles, yes Sir have another two large desks placed into this room across from mine. Charles Simply replied very good Sir it will be done.

Chapter 8: The Study

Pedro then asked Charles were there any areas you were not allowed to go. Well Sir you see you asked about areas of the castle and I told you there were none but you did not specify times. Times Pedro asked puzzled, what have times got to do with it. There was only one room I was not given access to unless I was called into it. "And where was that room Charles". It was here sir in this study, now your study. Sir I was only allowed to enter when called and it was usually something Sinure Alverez required. "What like Pedro continued". Well Sir he would sometimes ask for a hot drink or a cool drink or he might ask me to do some errand. "What drink was in the house", none Charles said sharply. None you mean there was no drink whatever at any time of year. None sir, the time of year was nothing to do with it. Señor Alverez did not drink and did not allow spirits into the castle. One year he was sent a 25-year-old scotch in an expensive wooden case from a friend of his. He told me to get the fire going which I did. He then took the bottle out throwing the elegant case on the fire! We watched the case burn then he told me to come with him and we went to the kitchen where he opened the bottle and I do declare that I felt quite joyful thinking of savouring the taste. He then emptied the bottle in its entirety down the sink. "Did you not question this, Charles"? No sir only in my mind I though what a waste of a great whiskey, however knowing Señor Alverez disapproved so strongly I said nothing. "What reasoning did you conclude from this action"? Well Sir I thought his strong Catholic faith prevented him from drinking and precluded me from bringing it into the castle. Oh, I see Pedro said, adding yes, I'm of the same opinion myself upon hearing what you have said. Were there any other incidents like this Pedro asked again. No Sir there were no other incidents of this nature or any other high strangeness. "Charles what did he do in his study". I was not allowed in here unless asked. I can honestly say that I have no idea except for the many letters he wrote. Letters Pedro prodded, yes Sir. How many times did you deliver these letters. Exactly none Sir. None? Yes, sir I never delivered a single letter or saw even as much as handled one envelope, however when I cleaned the grate in the fireplace Señor Alverez watched me intently. What did you think about this action. Sir I may be speaking out of turn but I deduced he may have had a lady friend and they were the musings of a letter to her followed by a change of heart. It also fits with his gambling visits which may be days at a time. Pedro said yes, yes, I see.

Charles where if anywhere did you not go in the castle Pedro again questioned? Señor Alverez's bedroom Sir. "Why is that"? Sir it would be so much easier to show you rather than tell you, please follow me. The pair climbed the spiral staircase and went into Señor Alverez's old bedroom. The was a four-poster bed with gold satin drapes adorning it. Under the window a heavy dark framed full-length mirror stood and to their left was a large oak drawered sideboard. Charles Face went ashen; his face was a ghostly pale as he gaped at the sideboard as though his face was frozen. "Is anything the matter Charles Pedro asked without real concern. Sir, Sir its gone. "What is gone"? Sir on this sideboard a Grotesk shrunken head used to stand in an expensive glass crystal case with facets down the sides which illuminated the thing even more. Oh Sir, five years I had to look at this thing when I was ordered to clean in here and every time I did, that pigmy with its pointed teeth and black dreadlocked hair. It would fill me with mortal fright and Sir now it has disappeared. Do you think Sir someone would play a trick on me Charles asked. Pedro though a moment then he said who would know this item would hold such fear for you? Sir no one knew of my anxiety about the thing, not even Señor Alverez. Ah I see, well that leaves just one thing to be done said Pedro. And Sir if I once again might be so bold, what is that? Put it out of your mind, treat it with the respect it deserves, dismiss it completely. Yes, Sir I shall do my best Charles said.

Chapter 9: Time Flies

Nearly a year passed without incident. Rose had bought the carriage from Pin Loe as agreed at the study. She had seen him several times since the meeting in the study with emphasis on being furtive. Again, she went to the bar and as she entered Pin Loe greeted her with a warm and charming smile. Hello rose my love. Rose smiled back and thought it might be a trap to place her off guard. Oh, pin she said it has been too long. Pin said yes it has, immediately he asked in a threatening voice "do you have any news for me". Rose cleared her throat and replied oh yes. Pin questioned tell me only about the last month.

Well, Rose said (she had rehearsed what she would say to Pin as she knew that questions would be coming). In the past month Pedro has become quite obsessed with gardening. I don't know whether it's his past love of the land and the soil or quite what it is. He is a strange man. Oh, I see said Pin in a confused voice, then asked have you ever slept with him. Rose indignantly splurted out I certainly have not, what would make you think of such a thing? I hope you have more faith in me than that.

Where does that leave us, Pin asked and I do not want to hear what you were unable to find out. I want to hear what you did find out. He has my money and the price will be more than he can afford I assure you. If you are wise you will think on this and your own future or lack of it. Rose agreed of course Pin. I will obey you to the letter. This is what you pay me for she said analytically.

Pin replied I do not pay you for misinformation, disinformation or no information. Looking at her with a scow crossing his lips.

Go back Rose and find something out of value. Return in your usual as soon as you know something of value as our next meeting will not be a pleasant one without information of value to me. Return and show comradery to Pedro and explain you have been to the market. Rose interjected saying and what do I take back. Pin looked at Link and said get her some vegetables. Link told Pin we have hardly enough for our own needs. Rose declared I do not wish to take the food you have. Pin stated we have more than we could possibly need - we could feed one hundred. Isn't that right Link, who answered it is sir. As Rose followed Link to the store room, they passed Pins office door which was ajar. And Rose immediately spotted Pins absent desk.

They returned with the vegetables which Rose refused. Pin seeing Rose had noticed his study uttered think nothing of it. Rose left the vegetables on the table and just as Rose reached the door she turned quickly and caught Pin unawares. Yes, rose he said in a strong voice. Rose wondered aloud. Pin where is your desk? There was brief pause then Pin finally answered. Oh, a man came in and offered me a price which will never come again so I surely took it. I am thinking of ordering a far larger desk and a very high-quality chair.

After Rose had left Pin visited his annoyance on Link. Why did you leave my study door open Link? I believe you were the last one out of my study this afternoon. Pin wanted to Blame him, berate him and scold him to the ends of the earth. Instead, he took a minute to compose himself and simply accepted things as they were adding Link, I will not forget this... my memory is long.

Link kowtowed to Pins wishes and gave the verbal surrender he had given so many times before. Link replied in the only way he could, I understand master and I was in the wrong and it will not happen again. It had better not Pin said with a murderous glint in his eye and running the outside edge of his forefinger across his throat. With that final admission from Link the conversation was ended.

Rose arrived at the castle laden with vegetables and made for the kitchen. Pedro grinned and teased with a question have you been on a day out somewhere. To which she answered yes, I have I have been to our favourite duck pond and sat in the afternoon sun but you were too busy to come. They all had their evening meal. Rose announced we will need to see you in the morning as soon as breakfast is over. Pedro asked is there something wrong? Rose merely replied oh nothing that will not keep until the morning with a hesitant laugh.

The church bell rang out as usual proclaiming it was eleven O clock. Breakfast was over when and the three of the went into the study. Pedro sat behind his big desk and said to what do we owe this occasion. Rose was the first to speak. Well Pedro as you will be aware at the end of the month the elections for Mayor will be fought. Pedro said yes what of it. Rose in full flow said we would like you to stand for Mayor as a candidate. Pedro said in a dark voice but I don't want to be a mayor of anywhere let alone here where I live!

Rose expected the rebuke and looked with a downtrodden attitude. Pedro asked please Charles will you please talk some sense into Rose. Charles replied Sir I cannot. Why Pedro insisted. Because she is wright Charles said with more authority than Pedro had heard from him before.

What makes you think I would have the first idea about how to be a mayor all I would be is a fraud and ultimately a failure. Pedro sounded off, your both fired and like a synchronized ballet dance they got up from their chair walking to the study door and turning the gold handles in unison to open it and continued with their heads held high. Just a minute Pedro said. Charles was the first to answer. I no longer work for you Sir he said. Rose added neither do I.

Oh, damn Pedro exclaimed. Come and sit down the pair of you and stop acting like children. They both did as they were bid. Pedro said now what's this all about. Rose took the lead and said you will be doing this community a disservice if you do not run for Mayor. How so Pedro asked. Charles interjected saying Sir can you imagine if Ping is the mayor and what the community would be like in three years' time. Pedro argued what has Pin Loe to do with anything and anyway the townships are not my problem. Charles replied no but they will be when you have been castigated, criticized and shunned by all the local towns.

Coming round Pedro asked them and how exactly is this to be achieved. Well sir we have drawn up plans as to how to move forward. Pedro said but the Mayoral Election is to be at the end of the month and Pin Loe would already have his campaign drawn up and will probably be putting the finishing touches to it. Precisely Rose interceded and that is why we must not waist a moment. Charles unrolled a large sheet of card on the desk. Sir he said these are the steps and the timings. Pedro thought his brain might explode but simply said you two have been plotting behind my back. Charles and Rose raised an eyebrow together. Right well Pedro announced what do I have to do first you pair of plotters. To which Charles replied Sir we are not plotters we are you right and left hands. Pedro had only heard a few French phrases in his life but one of them stuck with him so he replied "Touch e'" meaning you strike me with the tip of your sword. Charles was pleased at his vocabulary.

Right well Pedro announced what do I have to do first you pair of plotters. Well Sir Charles announced boldly. There has to a ball. Charles, have you taken leave of your senses man Pedro grumbled. Rose joined in and said Charles is wright to which Pedro replied oh you as well. What will it cost asked Pedro as Charles as he felt he was on a roll. Charles replied Sir I have it on good authority that your financial adviser has calculated all the figures and it will not impact our situation. Pedro feeling short tempered said Thank you indeed Charles and Rose for your efforts on my behalf.

Rose said the ball will be held in two weeks' time, invites shall be sent out to the dignitaries, the town council and the community in the local areas. Pedro wanted to know how they would get the invites printed in such numbers that and the décor are in hand and will be carried out in the Castle in time.

Charles went into his inside pocket and produced a gold invitation which read Greetings especially for you. Name of the intended receiver and this will be an occasion to be remembered. Free dining and drinks all evening. It was signed with Pedro' signature. Pedro looked dumbfounded. You two have been busy. The work will continue at eleven O clock tomorrow morning. Sir, please accept disruption to your usual work. Pedro fell on his desk with his arms cradling his head asking is there anything else I should know about?

I think that is about it except for the clothes Charles commented. Clothes Pedro said from his splayed fingers covering his eyes. Whatever can you mean. Charles continued well Sir we may have forgotten to mention that it is a ball of a fancy-dress nature which should not be missed at any price. Pedro relented feeling beaten... very well you two it shall be just as you said. Charles reminded him until eleven O clock tomorrow morning then Sir. Pedro dropped his hands said in acknowledgment until eleven then.

Chapter 10: Preparations

Ten O clock the following morning all were up dressed and anticipating a long day ahead. Pedro wished Rose a good morning. Charles Pedro said in a bright and cheerful voice a very good morning to you too. Continuing well, what to do Charles, who answered first things first Sir. A hearty breakfast will be served that will help us all. With that Charles disappeared into his kitchen while Rose worked rapidly on her figures. Charles quickly arrived with his usual silver tray laden with breakfast. Pedro commented you're a wonder Charles what time did you get up this morning. I began work at four O clock Charles replied. Pedro said what an ungodly hour to which Charles replied when needs must Sir, when needs must.

With breakfast over. Charles returned went into the study and immediately lifted the telephone receiver while Rose and Pedro worked away. I will be very busy today pointing down at the telephone told them. So, if you need to make calls, please use the one in the hallway or the one in the kitchen. Rose looked up and Charles had gone.

Then came a loud ringing sound from the bell pull rope outside. Rose got up and said cheerfully I'll get it. Pedro said get on with your work I shall answer the door. He was met by two burly men carrying a toolbox and two long ladders. Please do come in Pedro declared. Immediately the two men set to work scaling the ladders. Hammering and banging followed filling the void of the living room with echoes.

Another knock came to the door and again Pedro raised himself to his feet. Upon answering the door, he was surprised to see the coach driver facing him. In the delivery quarter Sir, he said streaming straight past Pedro who followed. The scullery door was open, in here sir the coachman asked. Then turned around and both went outside and began claiming the large hessian mail sacks containing blank invitations *the coachman* had earlier collected and placed them in the the back of the cart. Pedro recognized Roses handwriting and noticed the sacks had been labelled and tightly tied at the neck of each sack. They repeated the chore over and over until the cart was empty. At that the driver climbed aboard with haste and set off at incredible speed down the hill. So, it was the whole day as workmen, craftsmen and all manner of other visitors entered carried out their work and left.

The telephone rang in the afternoon. Pin said to Rose who answered thinking it was more workmen, get over here now without further ado and the receiver went dead. Rose said I have to go out, ball business I will be back later. The carriage waited outside as Rose climbed onboard. She was vigorously thrown backwards now the coach driver had returned. It was driven away with ferocity. Rose thought does he know anyone is in the coach clenching her fist and thumping the roof to which the coach speeded up. Soon the carriage door was opened and Rose somewhat dishevelled pulled her hands through her hair. as she walked towards the bar.

Chapter 11: The Master Sculptor

Entering she saw Pin stood by the bar announcing hello my lovely today is the day. Dear Pin how wonderful it is to see you I have missed you. Pin waved the greeting away and said now down to business my sweet. Right Pin said step behind the screen over there and change into the dress that link gives you. Somewhat confused and startled but this she did and then link led her by the hand to see herself in a full-length mirror behind the screen which had not been there a few moments earlier. Link held a dress out which she took and looked delighted holding it in front of her and observing the image in the mirror as the dress seemed to accentuate her hips and breasts. The dress clung to her curves as if it had just been tailored in the last hour. Alright I had this specially brought over from Paris; France pin announced. Rose excitedly said oh Pin I really do not know what to say. This is a gift I will treasure always.

He pointed at a chair in the middle of the room as she peeped over the screen saying sit down. She was escorted in by Link and was placed to catch the sun. Now Rose, what news have you to tell me Pin asked in an aggressive tone. Pin crossed the room with cat like speed and silence. While Pin moved with speed and agility and while she looked through the dirty bay window struck her without warning. Pin struck her again on both cheeks with equal measure. Hard enough to hurt and strong enough to make cheeks swell as the redness of her arteries filled them. Then followed two more vicious swipes from Pin as he struck Rose hard across again across both cheeks. Dazed Rose believed she could see in her mind's eye that she viewed a black sea rolling towards her then she fainted. But Link was lightning fast as his strong arms grabbed her around the waist and gently lowered her back into the chair. Well Pin told Link aloud so Rose could hear, there is very little happening up at the Castle at the moment. As she was beginning to come round Link said she lies, to which pin shouted do you think she has forgotten her obedience to me? Now Rose what news have you to tell me Pin asked once again in an aggressive tone

As she gradually recovered. A man entered. He was a master leather sculptor and artist. Pin had some trouble finding a craftsman of his skill. In a few minutes he had setup his easel and chair and was mixing paints on his wooden pallet. He then took a piece of charcoal and began tracing an outline. Pin gave him a broad smile whilst informing Rose do whatever he asks. Pin remarked oh don't worry she sometimes reacts like this to the heat. Slowly coming round, she said Pin we must talk as I have much to tell you. Pin replied so we shall my dear. Just follow instructions and all will be well.

There my dear much better. Standup he demanded which she did so without hesitation but felt a slight swaying motion in here body. Take two steps forward and stand perfectly still. Turn to the side Pin insisted, now the other side Pin persisted. Place your legs together and lower your head to your knees whilst gripping your ankles. Rose thought to herself I knew Pin was a strange man but this is bizarre even for Pin. She caught a glimpse of Link staring closely at her face and then her knees. Link poured her a glass of fresh cool water. Her brain was dizzy and she drained the water in one go. Link use a tailor's measure. Link continued completely checking the dress lengths and writing figures on a pad.

Pin walked up to her and she though he might strike her again. However, he gripped her jaw tightly turning her head first to one side then to the other. That done he pulled her face down then lifted her face toward the ceiling with four thin long like fingers finally returning her head to look straight at the artist.

The sculpture in lather was painted after being sat on the Mold The wet moulding technique worked beautifully in the sculptors' hands. It was beaten, shaved and expertly shaped as it was slowly wet leather moulded. Every rise and curve of the features had been conveyed to the Mold. Two hours later the sculptor artist declared there it is finished, please just leave it overnight to harden. Pin seemed pleased with the work that had been carried out simply saying it is a good likeness. Link stood between them with a bag of gold coins which he handed to the artist saying thank you for your service. Then he walked quickly to the door and opened it with his left arm while his right was displayed with an outstretched palm bidding the visitor farewell as he lowered it making a sweeping motion. The leather Master Artist left.

Now Pin asked Rose what is it you have to tell me, oh and it better be good! She had a look of fear in her eyes being alone with Pin. He's organizing a Ball on the 1st of November or el Día de Muertos. Pin Exclaimed the Spanish Day of The Dead. Is he mad? Everyone will be celebrating and no one will care about his ridiculous Ball. Rose continued well Pin you may be right as you so often are but it is not an ordinary Ball it is a Fancy-Dress Ball.

Pin showed great interest and asked how advanced are the preparations. She stated they are quite advanced but there are still many problems to be solved. Pin retorted excellent keep me updated on anything of importance. She said I will Pin, I will.

Unusually Rose' thoughts were muddled, cluttered and chaotic all at the same time. She said may I have a drink in your study. Pin said while hiding his annoyance, why yes surely. Link had returned and the three of them the entered Pins study. Rose was shocked as well as surprised but tried not to let it show on the face. What has happened to your desk, chair and where are all the books from the shelves you so much loved. Pin almost spilled his wine explaining. They are with my other treasured belongings. Pin went into an agitated state and furiously began pacing the room as if a military order he had given had been refused. His anger could be felt throughout the room and even Link was nervous at Pins demeanour. So, he took my fortune, he took my carriage, further he is trying to take what is mine, the mayorship of my town and now he has the audacity to take my dear Rose. Link nodded his head in agreement. Pin threw his glass at the wall in temper as it shattered in every direction. Rose thought for a moment then said but I am still here Pin and may I say I am here for you Pin and you alone. Pin simply said as the flush left his razor like cheeks. Very well, very well holding an outstretched arm indicating her visit was over.

The carriage stood waiting as she climbed aboard her thoughts raced trying to make sense of the afternoon but they tumbled around inside her head echoing off the walls of her mind during the journey back to the hotel as she slid from left to right in the carriage.

Chapter 12:Preparing for the Ball

The church clock chimed seven as they hurtled up the steep twisty road shortly arriving at the castle door. Rose once again composed herself as she thought of the time. Arriving shortly at the Castle door. Entering the living room, she said nonchalantly I am back in her most convincing voice. Charles greeted her and asked how was your afternoon Marm. Oh, of no consequence really Rose responded as she sat reading a tick list in her book.

The whole of the Castle outside had been painted in a brilliant white which carried a look of the DeVine against the skyline giving it something of a Heavenly quality. There was still lots of craftsmen who were busy up ladders, painting the curved staircase banister and completing the orchestras stage against the rear wall. While others were busy delivering extra chairs.

The next morning arrived somewhat early for the trio as they thought they had only been asleep for an hour and it was ready to go again. They filed down to a gratefully received breakfast with little or no chatter of the day that lay ahead. When breakfast was over. Charles went into the study and immediately lifted the telephone receiver while Rose and Pedro worked away. I will be very busy today pointing down at the telephone he told them. So, if you need to make calls, please use the one in the hallway or the one in the kitchen. Rose looked up and Charles had gone.

Hung above Rose and Pedro in the living room was a thirty-foot embroidered banner which had large lettering promoting the citizens of Spain and Pedro Sanchez for Mayor. Which hung from two strong ceiling mounts. Tables were laid out with every possible type of food. Chairs and sofas had been moved back to the walls opening up an even bigger space than the room than it already offered. A hastily but expertly built and decorated stage adorned the centre of the living room rear wall on which the orchestra tuned their instruments in readiness for the evening's celebrations.

Is it time for something to eat Charles, Pedro enquired. Indeed, it is sir they all sat down to a plate of sandwiches and Pedro said Well my left and right hand, today is the day. What say you, Charles? Charles replied indeed it is sir. And Rose what about you, everything is looking splendid and I say indeed it is sir, looking over at Charles with a cheeky grin pinned to her lips. Good, good, good Pedro said in an exalted cry. Time had passed. Many last moment deeds had been carried out and the time was now approaching seven O clock on the evening of the Ball!

Charles ordered Rose and Pedro to go to their rooms, wash and change in no later than thirty minutes. Without argument they both made haste up the circular staircase and duly with a minute to spare they arrived back in the living room. Charles commented Rose wherever did you get that dress. It makes you look more wonderful than you are if that is possible. Pedro wore a light blue suit which had a darker blue pattern on it which really made him look the part. Charles had gone for the new dark blue suit that Rose had recommended. He liked it because it made him look and feel like he was an adviser of some standing. All admiring one another's dress for the evening Charles said who is for champagne. Immediately Rose and Pedro raised a hand in the air and Charles produced his personal monogrammed silver tray with the drinks on it.

Charles asked Sir shall I offer the orchestra one. They were studiously tuning their instruments to which Pedro's reply was why not and asking Charles, have we got enough to go around for the whole evening? Charles replied with a smile; indeed, we have Sir. Charles offered the orchestra a drink of chilled orange juice each which they took most gratefully. We don't want you worse for wear Charles told them and they all laughed.

Chapter 13: Death at the Ball

Guests began to arrive in numbers. The coach driver had been warned by Pedro, if you wish to keep your position. Yes, Sir I do the coach driver exclaimed for the first time with a hint of panic in his voice. Yes, Sir whatever you need the driver replied. Well, you had better understand this and you had better understand it well. Sir the driver nodded. I realize you are very pushed for time as we all are but hear me now and hear me clearly you need to bring guests to the Castle safely and not rolled about like some more mail bags. Do we understand each other Pedro asked to which the driver said Yes Sir it will be done exactly as you say. We will see Pedro said one complaint just one and I will hire a new driver. The driver said I understand Sir, I understand. to which Pedro added tonight is not a game. The driver departed at the fastest speed he dare.

Pedro returned to the Castle and saw Rose. Everything alright he asked. Charles everything alright? Rose and Charles looked at each other and raised any eyebrow almost simultaneously. Charles was the first speak Pedro this is your night everything is ready, get rid of those nerves everything is fine.

An hour and a half later guests began to arrive in numbers and Charles was the convivial host offering the guests Champaign. Soon they were joined by more and more guests. A corner of the living room was beginning to fill up. Then Charles looked around the room and estimated there was two hundred guests of which eighty was present. He went on his second round with drinks as the orchestra played a favourite tune known by most in Spain. There were couples dancing people drinking and people eating.

Charles asked may I introduce you to Maria Catalina who is the present Deputy Mayor or Junta de Gobierno Local. Maria acknowledged the introduction with a wave of her hand saying oh thank you. Pedro and Maria discussed the future of the Mayorship and appointment of a new deputy Mayor. They got on so well and their ideas for Mayor were in total alignment. Charles moved on to mingle with other important dignitaries. He was pleased at the rapport between them and seeing Pedro handling his job so well. So, the introductions went on and on until they had dwindled to anyone who was anyone.

He felt so much more comfortable as he left for his kitchen. Collecting more Champaign, he loaded up his tray and turned as he did so he glanced out of the corner of his eye seeing what he believed resembled a large cat on the Castle wall. It stopped in the shadow of the tree behind it. Charles shook his head and thought no more of it.

He placed the Champaign on one of the tables. No sooner had he done so than the hordes descended on them. One man had taken it upon himself to serve the nectar himself choosing women only at first. Charles thought saves me a job.

A hooded would-be intruder slipped the iron key from his pocket into the heavy front door lock and it turned easily as a metallic sound emanated from the inner mechanism. Trying the door, it opened and swung slightly back on its large frame. The intruder slipped through, locked the door behind him and moved behind the crowds of guests.

Swiftly moving onto the circular staircase stopping momentarily in a large patch of shadow. Surveying the living room the intruder moved on with speed and agility. Then making a slow move to one of the many windows on the back wall. Opening one of the windows was something dark and small slid through hiding behind the full-length drape which hung at the side of the window.

The heavily hooded and caped intruder went and stood looking down on the gathering. No one seemed to notice him except Charles. Who handed his beloved silver tray to Pedro then moved with a speed befitting a man ten years younger. He Sprang up the spiral staircase taking three steps at a time. As he reached the top, he noticed one of the crossed rapier swords had been removed from its mount. Charles instinctively took the other one and launched himself onto the ceiling level floor to which he was greeted by the swivelling caped intruder who said nothing but taking a defensive stance and raising the rapier in a threatening manner.

The intruder then Lunged forward at Charles and Charles who moved immediately to the post which was a move requiring much skill and by doing this blocked the thrust. The fight was in earnest. The pair duelled with post, lunges, cuts and thrusts. Charles thought to himself between lunges, parrying and countering cuts and thrusts, I wasn't the seven times champion fencing master at a private school for nothing. He made a fade just as the intruder lunged and put his rapier through his opponents' guard as fast as he was able. faster than the intruder could counter, Charles twisted his rapier and withdrew it with incredible strength speed. Charles realized his   ploy of a fade had worked as the intruder's blade was caught up in his hand guard so with lightening reactions Charles twisted and withdrew his Rapier allowing the deadly blade to fall behind him.

The Rapier left the intruders hand and a sudden thought struck him. Moving without thinking at speed the assailant dived over the balcony rail. Gripping the banner there was a loud Ooh from the guests below. Still sliding down the banner the intruder gripped the banner both hands as he came to its end still thirty feet from the floor. The banner was now swinging wildly toward the wooden carved statue of Jesus. The intruder used both feet in a violent kick forcing it away with an aggression and ferocity which made the statue fly backwards to its maximum height nearly hitting the glass dome above. The intruder with the force also flew backwards to the same degree. The swing of the banner and the statue gathering speed made the meeting of the two was likened to two opposing pendulums hurled at each other. Upon their clash into each other the statues feet caught the intruder full in the stomach. Releasing the banner the intruder desperately clung onto the statue's legs. Having the wind forced out of the intruder's body meant full strength was not there to grip any longer. He was suddenly hurtling downwards until he landed on the couch against the wall. The crowd drew back seeing the caped hooded intruder spring from the couch, apparently unhurt by the fall then landing on the marble floor before making his way straight for the study. The intruder had fled hotly pursued by several Civil Guards

Charles was still trying to get through the throng of guests. Charles returned to the ball room floor and making for the study as guests stood in his way. Entering he asked what's that. Pedro still had both feet firmly holding a wriggling mass on the floor in place. Don't know Pedro answered. Have you seen Rose in a long while? Charles said. Now you come to mention it I haven't seen her since early evening. Charles raised his head and looking upwards pronouncing Lordy, lordy this does not bode well sir.

Just then the study opened and Captain Valdez entered I am sorry to tell you, without pausing he stated I am sorry to bring bad news. Continuing he told Pedro the intruder has been caught and is positively identified as Miss Rose your assistant. What! Pedro shouted. Then this cannot be. As he got up from the couch, he grabbed the thing that was below him dragging it with him. Just as they reached the study door and an appendage from the creature felt for anyway of escape. Captain Valdez went through the study door followed by Pedro who was still dragging the mass behind him.

Captain Valdez knelt down beside of the intruders and said its Rose alright. Pedro knelt at the other side of the body. Valdez lifted the hood slightly back to reveal Roses features. Valdez continued it is your assistant all right. Dumbfounded but still not letting go of the creature from the study Pedro looked shocked. Valdez said and I'm sorry she was a lovely woman but people change. Pedro shouted wait, wait, wait there is something wrong here. Valdez said the proof is there before us. Pedro said as he opened the cloak revealing the same dress and shoes that Rose the been wearing earlier that evening and pointed at the dress. So, what Captain Valdez asked. So, this Pedro said removing the perfect mask of Rose moulded on the face and revealing Pin Loe underneath it. Valdez said I don't believe it; well, I do believe it but how much effort went into creating this monstrosity. Valdez made the sign of the cross looking up at the statue of Jesus which hung above them. The thing that Pedro had gripped by the fur suddenly saw its chance for escape. Six armed Federalises stood in the hallway blocking the door caught him by the fur. While Captain Valdez said what next, is it to be Frogs or Locusts of the seven plagues, then the creature was dumped to the side of Pin Loe. Valdez and Pedro again knelt either side of them. Valdez was the first to spot the zipper which he unzipped revealing Link dressed in a perfectly made monkey outfit.

Valdez was rarely lost for words in his usual way of being only too full of praise for himself, but this was one time when he had none. Right take them both away he commanded. They were removed and Valdez stated once again how sorry he was for such an incident to take place. He added no need to inform my superiors I will do that as I have to write a detailed report of the incident. Yes, Captain Valdez said Pedro agreeing. The next quarter of an hour saw all the guests filtering away murmuring how eventful the evening had been. Comments ranged from this kind of entertainment cannot be got at any price, how good the food was or the generosity of the drink. One older female guest added I would definitely come again.

Captain Valdez said you may wonder Pedro about Pin. You may not know Pedro but mistakes happen, I myself was once part of a misunderstanding. Pedro wondered what he was trying to say.

Valdez said there was a gambler who told me that I had been cheating, however he changed his mind, accepted his mistake in telling Pin of his accusation and had had made a grave mistake which would never be repeated. Myself and Pin just looked at each other and smiled. At the time Valdez continued the delay got the gathering gamblers muttering about their expectations of outcomes with enthusiasm in one anticipated yet low noise. Pin realised how the wait had made the gamblers keener that ever to re-start proceedings and so that's what he did and the game was continued. Pedro had no idea why he had been told or what Valdez was getting at by revealing mistakes happen. After the evenings events Valdez must know his admonition was totally inappropriate but just replied I thank you so much for being honest with me. I believe we will all sleep sounder in our bed tonight because of the way you have dealt with this incident. Both men shook hands and the evening' episode was closed. Valdez said in his most friendly tone. With that Captain Valdez left following his men with the arrested Pin and link between them.

Has anyone seen Rose Charles asked? Pedro said I will search downstairs and you check upstairs. Will do Charles shouted a reply to him climbing the staircase. Rose, rose he shouted as he neared the top of the stairs. Pedro suddenly shouted from the kitchen doorway. Charles panic over she is here. Charles could hardly believe his eyes as he entered the kitchen. Four empty bottles of Champaign lay on the kitchen table. Rose was slumped forward in Charles chair. Shall I take her to her bedroom Sir Charles asked? Pedro said yes do that please Charles.

The morning after the evening's events Rose said finally at the kitchen table in a squeaky low voice, I'm sorry, I'm sorry, oh why don't you say what's on your mind? Charles and Pedro looked at each other as Pedro said I thought excluding the incident with Pin, the Ball went off perfectly, would you agree Charles. He replied indeed I would Sir my thoughts exactly. Rose looked at her plate knowing they were being kind and then thinking about the absurdity she must have displayed during the latter part of the evening just broke out laughing, Pedro and Charles joined in and all three laughed. What happened Rose Pedro asked. Well, she replied I went into the kitchen and was suddenly grabbed by the throat, forced into your larder in your chair Charles. The assailant started pouring campaign, whisky and I don't know what else down my throat as quick as they could. Right then Pedro said we will bring you up to date on last evening' events and then we shall leave it where it belongs – in the past. All nodded in agreement. Charles said I was thinking of doing some work in the garden today, would anyone like to join me. Two hands were raised in the air and breakfast was over. Rose sat and read the El Conciso newspaper in which the headline read Well Known Master Sculptor found dead in pond near his home. Shocked, Rose thought about her peculiar meeting with Pin, Link and the Sculptor. It had been a puzzle, buried in a maze and wrapped in a mystery and she believed they were part of it. The newspaper article suggested otherwise surmising his death was most likely accidental. Stating it is yet to be determined if this was nothing more than a drink fuelled misadventure.

The door bell rang but no one was there. As Charles opened the front door, he saw he had received mail. It had him mystified. A gold card announced that three extra guests would be arriving on Saturday evening and six of chairs should be laid out in a semicircle in front of Pedro' desk at.an arm's length apart. He would be very wise to carry out these instructions exactly as demanded in this message. No food or drink would be necessary as attendance by all would be enough.

Rose, Charles, Pin, Link, Captain Valdez and Pedro all had a gold invitation to the Alverez castle. Each had its own personal message that was to be kept secret. The invitations read SIX BULLETS. You know what you did! If you are wise and do not want me to share your dirty secret with the world and everyone in it you will be prompt and do exactly as you are told on the evening in question. All recipients were puzzled by this personal hand delivered message. They saw no one delivering the message. Each of them thought how could anyone know of their past. This was preposterous and outrageous but it was enough to get all of them to attend.

Duly Saturday arrived Six chairs sat arranged in the study in a semicircle Infront of Pedro's large desk. All were seated and looked at each other with disbelieving eyes and a sense of fear wondering if they might be the one that was chosen. The only empty chair was the last one for Pedro. Rose looked at Charles and without making a sound nodded at the empty chair. Charles looked at it and then back at Rose whilst shaking his head.

In the Darkness suddenly one of the bookshelves slid silently slightly out and to the side. Only five of you are gathered, are you going to tell me where Pedro is. Charles face had gone ashen, Captain Valdez took his cap off and lowered it to his chest, Rose eyes widened, Señor Alverez spoke loudly and clearly from behind Pedro's desk. Greeting them with a thank you for coming. Alverez took centre stage saying well as he looked at the sixth empty chair? Rose said please tell us who you are and what you want with us?

They all looked at each other without speaking. Then Rose spoke up again. We last saw him this morning, he had bought me a new gardening implement called a trowel. Charles was two rows across from me and was working hard digging the soil. Pedro came out of the Castle walking to the carriage and shouted I will be back quite late, I'm off to buy seeds from the stores. We shouted goodbye to him and have not seen him since Rose declared.

Has anyone anything to add to this Alverez said. No one spoke. This gathering is not complete until he arrives Alverez told them. Alright as Rose has asked about me. I shall tell you. I know each of you better than you know yourselves. My background was as an intelligence officer in the Spanish army and I was recognised as the best in the whole intelligence core. I worked my way up to Colonel. I went to many countries posing as this, that or the other. I visited all parts of Spain carrying out my duty. I was only known as the 'Dagger'. If struck fear in the hearts of those who were to be assassinated irrespective of position, rank or gender. I lost count of how many beautiful deaths after I killed twelve men and six women. But that's all a long time ago, there have been many who felt my blade since then and they have all paid the ultimate price so any of you would be heroes should take note. I will kill you before you reach this desk.

The silence was all engulfing and his threat had its desired effect upon the small gathering, Señor Alverez continued with his captive audience. Be patient it will all over soon enough but don't let impulse or desperation make it sooner than it needs to be. I am an expert in getting information from anyone. No one can hide from me. I can do it by money or force. The choice is entirely theirs; they can be the master of their own fate or not as the case maybe. It makes it easier for me if the target holding this information does it for payment but it does cut short my pleasure. If they chose not to tell me then my methods would make them tell me more information that I need. You see death is a choice just like any other.

Charles then spoke out saying Señor Alverez I don't understand why you have said "you see death is a choice just like any other", are you unwell Señor Alverez? Thankyou Charles I am both well as ever can be and I will kill someone this night.

Charles stated Sir whoever you are I deplore this kind of behaviour or speech because I have known you for five years but Sir, I earnestly implore you to think carefully before you say another word. Alverez said thank you Charles My loyal servant to the last. I like that Alverez said. However, he did not like it. He felt Charles' reply was not part of the death script which he had in his head. Charles and all of you gathered here tonight should be asking yourselves one thing only, will I be a survivor! You may believe my name is Alverez or whatever pleases you, it matters not. I have told you I am thee master of disguise. Charles you are a fool.

Continuing with his persona Señor Alverez said I need your attention, when every eye was completely on him. He was in his element as the starring role he had given to his victims so many times, like a great actor in a stage play. In all his life he felt he was the drama in life and that he alone controlled and could create the world that would be without this person or that woman. He was omnipotent. He alone could grant life or death without pity or mercy for his victims. Alverez felt he was a god who roamed far and wide murdering with impunity, no remorse, only a sense of achievement. The greatest pleasure he had was taking a life! It would excite him, his patience was controlled until the moment he carried out his evil reckoning, it was almost like a sexual act which would always end in a climax leaving him drained and elated at the same time.

Rose glanced over to Charles with a worried look while wondering what Alverez was going to say next. Who is this Señor Alverez Charles thought. Charles said we all know it is you Señor Alverez as the rest nodded in agreement. Charles thought he must try to reach him by saying his belief that Señor Alverez was indeed not well and all could attest to that. Señor Alverez looked at the gathered guests, laughed loudly and then said you poor fools, so you all think I am Señor Alverez, with a wave of his hand declaring anyway no matter.

While they all looked on with incredulity, Charles said but Sir I worked for Señor Alverez for five years, I know who he is and what he looks like! Indeed, you do not Charles, I took you in like all the others. Beggin, you pardon Sir are you trying to say the past five years have been a lie. That would be impossible. I would have known. Bravo Charles were you aware of my every movement. No Sir I was not. Sir if you don't mind me saying I trusted you from the start. How could you now betray your trust in me? It was not my place to question you and your movements. I thank you Charles for your misplaced devotion over the last five years. Charles was stunned into silence. This had been the barrage that had closed him down. In one final attempt he said but Señor

Alverez please say you are having a joke and this is all a jape Sir. This is no Joke Charles; it is anything but. The more serious you take me the better your chances of survival.

Charles needed to draw breath and all stretched in every possible way to look at him whilst doing so. Sir I have one question only he stated. I believe we all have the right to know who I have been addressing for the past five years? Señor Alverez told him. You have been addressing whomever I decided to become. Charles argued but Sir I would have known. Señor Alverez replied why are you some kind of an expert on intelligence matters?

Charles said Sir you are being unreasonable! "Why". Well, if you are not who you have said you are then that would mean you had to fool all of us which would not have been possible. Dear loyal Charles Alverez replied you have no idea who I am, none of you have, I am a master of manipulation, Impersonation and ultimately death! Charles was annoyed but controlled his feelings thinking if this is true, I was indeed taken for a fool. He had been lied to and duped. Believing everyone in the room must feel the same as him. However, he felt gratified as he had spoken his mind.

Just then Señor Alverez took a gun out of his pocket. He aimed it deliberately and with menace at each individual seated before him then he told them, all or some of you may survive. Señor Alverez looked at each of them with a piercing stare and told them, all or some of you may die, it matters not to me one way or the other, he delighted in the fact that he knew none had a chance of survival. He would shortly murder them all. Addressing them all he said you will not interrupt me while I tell you the charges laid out before me.

we come to you dear Rose. You killed both your parents by slashing your mothers throat and stabbing your father to death three times then running away. "You are guilty as charged". Rose just looked down into at her lap. The others looked horrified at her.

Let me tell you the sordid story of Pin. Pin had been a prison guard at an internment camp in Beijing until one day the opportunity presented itself, he was stood in a grave for a prisoner who had literally died of starvation. Ping Loe was seen to have worked digging the grave furiously. The commandant smiled and told him what a good party member he was and he would put this in his report to the commissioners. Pin stepped out of the grave laid his shovel over his shoulder swinging a deadly blow from its edge hitting the commandant with a force that almost severed the head clean off. He buried the commandant' body deep in the grave alongside the other prisoner. After filling the makeshift grave in again, he then had a shed moved to sit on top of the grave Pin Loe went back to the commandant' office immediately changing from his uniform for the commandant' spare uniform. He was very aware during August of the pressures of the Sino-French war in 1884 in the South East of China and Pin took advantage of it.

He eased into the role of commandant and the other guards had no choice but to accept the old commandant's decision in choosing Pin. The commissioners wrote to him and asked to get the numbers of prisoners down. The cost of running the internment camp was too high. They told him you have been recommended they did not tell him by whom but instead said in their communication you need to prove your worth. Get the numbers down. Pin knew the prison was grossly overcrowded and knew the War would be having an impact in all quarters. He thought fighting for the sovereignty of Vietnam was the reason that cuts needed to be made in all of China' internal structures, whether they were directly related or not. The Message was as far as he was concerned save the government money for them to be able to oust the French from the Indochina regions formed by Vietnam and constituting Annam, Tonkin and Cochinchina which became the Siamese kingdom of Cambodia and Laos sometime later.

He pulled out every paper about appointments. Then took out a sheet of headed paper with the prison office official stamp on it along with the old governor's signature and began writing to the commissioners. He stated he as commandant' required a complete change and was going away and would not be returning. The resignation letter went on to say he recommended an appointee who had shown excellent qualities for the past six years. And so, the letter to the commission went on extoling the virtues of one Pin Loe. The appointment was sanctioned one week later. Pin Loe ran a tight ship and told all guards that what was needed was discipline the camp had become lax. Any prisoner or for that matter guard broke the rules would be dealt with in the most severe manner which meant a swift death. Also, false accusations would be dealt with in the strongest terms. His falsified the letter to the commissioners for choice of commandant stated that the outgoing commandant was leaving due to ill health and that they would do well to accept his nomination of Pin Loe Chun was an exceptional choice. One day Pin was informed of a new prisoner who was known as a Master Magician. Pin told a guard to bring him to me now. The magician was offered a chair, a cigar and a glass of strong drink. Pin told him this is how it can be or the alternative is if I am displeased you will be tortured each and every day you do not teach me a new trick. The Magician replied but Commandant I am only skilled in card tricks and sleight of hand. Well Pin said you will have to make them the best I have ever seen. Six months past and Pin and the magician took their usual walk by the pond. Pin concealed knife walking slightly behind and checking there were no prisoners anywhere around as they were not allowed outside at this time and no guards were present. He grabbed the prisoner's forehead and slashed the magician across the throat.

Later the next day in an assembly yard meeting Pin called the death of the starved prisoner had been from one of the frequent prisoner fights and those responsible would be very sorry. The assembled guards all nodded in acknowledgement. Pin said now moving on we are very lucky to have our minister arriving later this week and I want everything to look like new. A low murmur of yes went through the guards. That is all for today and remember what I have said about the prisoner who died. Pin Loe stepped down from his makeshift podium.

One-week later commissioner Chen arrived. All the guards had been assembled and Pin stood on a newly made podium. Speaking about the need to keep and restore discipline. Pin clapped followed by the guards. After a half hour it was all over and Pin walked Chen through the grounds on this warm pleasant morning. Pin asked him if he would like a cool drink brought out to him no Chen said just it has to be a shorter visit than I would have liked as I have several other appointments today. He asked how do you like your post? And it's not too tiring, is it? Pin immediately wondered where the conversation was leading. I like the post very much commissioner. Chen almost reading his thoughts said I only ask because the commissioners insist on good treatment for commandants, guards and prisoners alike. Pin stated and we party members are most grateful to the party and the commissioners for their interest, support and generosity. With that the commissioner swivelled on his heel and walked back through the main gate and left.

Pin left the prison heading for the Port of Tanguu. The train journey was long and arduous until he finally arrived in Tanguu in the midafternoon. Pin looked into the depths of the Tanguu harbor, then the thought of killing his old governor and an inmate in the Beijing internment camp flowed over him like the crooked smile that crossed his face.

Now we come to you Link who threw a man overboard to slowly drown. Then you murdered a now famous artist in a local pond. You carried out Pins instructions over time and murdered many men in a deadly gambling challenge. You are guilty as charged.

Alverez then moved his piercing gaze from Link to Captain Valdez stating there have been many deaths since you have entered Spain Alverez announced. Your first murder was when you had been accused of cheating by a gambler at one of Pins challenge nights. The gambler however was unaware of the agreement you had with Pin. if he did not keep up payments to you your protection would stop. You are both corrupt and a murderer. The gambler who accused you was taken into your jail and three days later was weighted down then thrown over the harbour wall. You are guilty as charged.

Shall we play a game? No one said anything, continuing Alverez said good so we are all agreed. This game is called "DEATH CARD" and if you were wondering ace is low, He took a pack of cards out of his pocket and all seated looked with an intense stare. Alverez shuffled the pack like a master then fanned them out held them in one hand pointing them slightly down. His other hand waved the pistol in their direction. Ah I see I have your undivided attention. He walked over to Charles then said pick a card. Everyone looked at Charles' face as Alverez said take you card and place it face down in front of you between your feet. Charles followed Alverez's 'instruction. Now he said we come to the lovely Rose who did the same by choosing a card and placing it on the floor between her feet face down. This continued until all five of them had a card between their feet.

Alverez went through the cards one at time searching for the most important of the cards which was the six of spades. He became frustrated and began waving his pistol at them again. Has any of you taken a card from my deck. All five of the shook their head. Alverez was beside himself with a red-faced anger that even Charles had not seen before. Alverez was perturbed so he drew the seven of clubs and placed it face down where Pedro was to be seated when he arrived.

Ace is equal to a one, and so on Alverez declared. This my dear murders are your death numbers saying alright you may turn you card over. Charles drew the two spades; Rose had the ace of spades while Pin had the three and four was held by link leaving Captain Gonzalez with five of spades.

Alverez reiterated Ace is low or a one for the non-gamblers amongst you which is Charles. I have to tell you that this is a game of death. Charles suddenly erupted with, the comment you mean to kill us by an order of a card Charles you are the fool you have been for the past five years. As its name suggests so I will tell you this the number you have will represent your death in order. Shall we turn Pedro's card over. Oh, seven of clubs, that means he gets to watch you all die before he finally is dealt the same fate himself.

Now where is Pedro? Señor Alverez said it is so rude to be late for your own death party. Well let me see now, we have a little time to fill in so where was I oh yes. My name if you are wondering is Carlos Rodrigo and I was the colonel in charge of the intelligence department of the Spanish army. So, I have a little time to fill. I will tell you what Pedro Sanchez did due to his temporary absence. A starving man came to his farm to beg a piece of bread. Pedro told him he would get him some then took the pitch fork from behind the door and stabbed it into the man's chest. He then battered his face to a pulp with a shovel so he could not be recognised and disposed of the body. He turned up here, and the rest you know. Carlos Rodrigo said shall we get on with the proceedings raising the gun. Saying goodbye Rose don't worry all of your turns will come.

Rose my love did Pedro say anything to you about tonight? She replied not a single word. Oh, rose you are such a disappointment to me and to many others, some of whom lay rotting in their grave like your parents. You put them there and now you have the chance to do the right thing and tell me what Pedro said to you this morning. Silence followed. Alverez moved his investigation to Charles. Ah Charles you are to be trusted more than the rest, we have known each other for so very long and perhaps one could describe it as being friends. Please Charles tell me did Pedro tell you anything about this evening or the invitation which may shed some light on things as to why he is so very late. Replying Charles said, taking all of his bravado "Alverez", I have nothing to tell you not because I will not but because I cannot as he did not say a single word which would give even the faintest clue as to the invitation, his lateness or any reason but I wish he was here now. Alverez said you and me both Charles. Then Charles shouted at the top of his voice your mad! We have all told you all we know. Alverez said I believe you Charles. Maybe he will not turn up at all. So, we will have our fun without him.

Rose You dear, dear lady I am an excellent shot and I have never been known to miss. So, I am going to shoot you so your bile gets into your blood stream. The only way to explain this is that you will be in such indescribable agony as the poison from your own body flows around you which means when the agony becomes too much to bear but takes its time to kill you and you are aware all the time it is your own body which is killing you slowly. Your friends if they care for you will not be able to stand your screams and will have to gag you. Alverez raised his pistol as Charles shouted you can't shoot Rose as he Pleaded for her life; this is cold blooded murder!

Just then the secret passage door was opened quickly and silently. Pedro stood at the top of the steps with his old gun from the challenge and the sixth bullet which had never fired. He stood in the centre of the doorway and whistled. Alverez whipped round with lightning speed pulling his trigger. The bullet from his gun lodged in the stone steps of the secret passage. Pedro's bullet was aimed directly to the heart of Alverez, who fell stone dead on the desk.

Clapping erupted from all as Pedro collected his boots from the second step of the passage and walked over and sat on the front of his desk as he pulled his boots on. I think we might have to address one more thing. The clapping stopped and Pedro said we are all witnesses to what happened here tonight and in the eyes of the law we are all responsible as the courts would deem it murder by association even if you did not commit the act personally. Is that not correct Charles Pedro asked? Actually, Sir the law is quite clear on this point however there may be extenuating circumstances which may mean you receive reduced but non the less significant jail time. They would be likely to hang us slowly and surely one and all.

Pedro Added as you all know it was me who killed him pointing at the body. However, I have to tell you the Civil Guard have their ways. We all need to think because if one of us goes down, we all go down. As a Civil Guard prisoner, one of you maybe be the Judas goat because you cannot take the torture any longer. Standing trial would mean death for us all. I do not ask you to do this for me but rather for yourselves. The five of them muttered between themselves when Padro suddenly spoke up. Firstly, is there anyone who wants to risk the army colonel's shooting in a military court room hearing. Or would you rather take your chances in a Civil Courtroom. Or perhaps with the newspapers getting their readers clambering for our blood. People will want to kill us in the street without knowing any of the facts.

Captain Valdez said Pedro speaks the truth it maybe he has an understanding of Civil Guard methods to achieve their goal, which will be to send us to our deaths as slowly and painfully as possible "So I'm in", Link and Pin echoed their words together "were in". Rose said "oh yes" as Charles shouted "absolutely". Pedro said resolutely, that leaves me and my answer is a firm "Yes". None of us should enter into this pact unless we they are completely determined to keep our secret until the end of our lives! The issue now facing us all is how do we dispose of the body?

He continued we have a very deep well out in the back garden which has been covered over to make it safe. We must uncover it, tie some heavy rocks around the body and very importantly each one of us must hold a piece of the Spanish flag on which he is covered. Then together we tip him into his watery grave. We will then "all" get more large rocks and throw them down the well until they just break the water level, so as to make it appear filled in. Any amount of searching will reveal nothing. If your mind is made up on this, we make a pact this night that none of us will ever break. If any of you has the slightest doubt in their mind now is the time to say it. Total silence followed as Pedro said with conviction, "Place your right arm out and place your hand palm facing down on top of each other's hand! Soon all except Pedro' were stacked one upon the other. Finally, his hand sat on top of the other's, saying repeat after me, "I swear by almighty god that I make this pact with my heart and soul this night, Amen".!

The next day the deed was duly done and all contributed to carry out the task. They retired to the main living room and sat and drank Champaign all afternoon. Pedro told them you may all go back to doing whatever you want now and good luck to you all. Questions like what will you do now, will you move and other such small talk pervaded the air. Pedro Charles asked what if the old challenge gun had not fired? There was a silence in the chatter as intense interest grew in the answer. In that circumstance then Pedro said, dragging it out further well in that event... We would all be dead. The gathering roared with laughter.

One year later a marriage was announced between Pedro and Rose. Charles was to be the best man. Pin was to drive the bride's carriage. Link followed with instructions to drive Pedro slowly in his new specially decorated carriage. Pin was unceremoniously told to drive in the most casual manner missing holes in the road and delivering the bride in a state of total relaxation. Captain Valdez had brought extra men to make up a guard of honour while the usual coach driver handed out prayer books and greeted everyone as they entered.

Epilogue/Conclusion

Six could be killers. One of them could be a serial killer. What is needed is to understand the characters, their motivations and the pressures each of them face. Having a clear understanding of the events, characters and motives if there are any is the key to unlocking the mystery.

Bibliography

The Society of Authors

University Library

Pan MacMillan

ASK

Yahoo

Library Archives

Quora

The Publishers Marketplace

Microsoft Bing

Amazon

Linked In

Reddit

Yandex

DuckDuckGo

Baidu

Facebook

YouTube

Google

Acknowledgments

I truly do not know what inspired me to write this novel. It came to me at night and continued as the characters became more rounded. Did this ever happen. Was this a true story. The honest answer is… Who knows. Maybe a band of disparate and desperate characters assembled from all corners of the globe to unite in predetermined circumstances.

About the Author

The Author is above all a thinker. He has a university degree and has visited every classroom in the school of life. A consummate professional with many achievements. The author attended an ordinary secondary modern school. He is a single man, the oldest of four children and his interests are as broad as the cosmos.